The Mercenary

THE LIBRARY OF BANGLADESH

MOINUL AHSAN SABER

The Mercenary
A Novel

TRANSLATED BY SHABNAM NADIYA

CALCUTTA LONDON NEW YORK

Seagull Books, 2018

Original © Moinul Ahsan Saber, 2016

Translation © Shabnam Nadiya, 2016

ISBN   978 0 8574 2 500 3

THE LIBRARY OF BANGLADESH series was conceived by
the Dhaka Translation Center at the University of Liberal Arts Bangladesh.
Find out more at http://dtc.ulab.edu.bd/

Printed in arrangement with Bengal Lights Books

This edition is not for sale in Bangladesh

British Library Cataloguing-in-Publication Data
A catalogue record for this book is available from the British Library

Typeset and designed by Sunandini Banerjee, Seagull Books, using artwork
by Narottama Dobey and W. Basher from the Bengal Lights editions
Printed and bound by Maple Press, York, Pennsylvania, USA

•

LIBRARY OF BANGLADESH
An Introduction

The independence of Bangladesh, while into its fifth decade now, is still viewed by many outsiders as an accident of history. All historical outcomes are in part an accident, but any event of the magnitude of Bangladesh's liberation can only happen as a consequence of deep and long-term agency. What underlies that agency in this case most decisively is a unique cultural identity.

Like the soft deposits flowing down from the Himalayas that created the land mass known as Bangladesh today, its culture too has resulted from centuries of diverse overlay. Generations here have always gravitated towards the mystical branch of the reigning faith, be it Buddhism, Hinduism or Islam. The net effect is a culture that has always valued tolerance and detachment over harsh rituals or acquisitive fierceness.

There is no way better than Bangladesh's literature to know what makes this unique and vital culture as full as it is of glory and, of course, foibles. How did a rain-washed delta full of penniless peasants turn into a leader among developing nations? How did the soft, mystical, Baul-singing population turn into one of the fiercest guerilla armies of the last century? How did love of the Bangla language trigger the very march to freedom? How do the citizens of the world's most densely populated city, barring only a few tax or gambling enclaves, make sense of daily life, and find any beauty, amid all the breathless din of commerce and endless jostle of traffic?

The first three books in this series provide a remarkable window into the realities and mindscape of this amazing, confounding, rich world through translations of three of the living legends of Bangladeshi writing: Syed Shamsul Haq, Hasan Azizul Huq and Syed Manzoorul Islam. The presentation of their work has been made possible by the Dhaka Translation Center, hosted by the University of Liberal Arts Bangladesh. It also owes a great deal to the tireless efforts of its Director, Kaiser Haq. The series owes most, however, to award-winning translator Arunava Sinha, who both helped conceive of this idea, and helms it as series editor. Eminent translators brought together by him have ensured a rare and truly world-class rendition of these hidden gems of world literature. The impressive international-standard production owes everything to DTC's sister concern, Bengal Lights, led by editor Khademul Islam and managing editor, QP Alam.

Bangladesh, for all its success, is still to the world the sum of half-told stories told by others. It's high time to offer a fuller account of ourselves to the world. DTC plans to bring out at least three titles each year, and add both new names and new titles by selected authors to this defining series on Bangladeshi writing. We also believe that the process of consciously engaging new and wider audiences will lead to new refinements to a body of work that is already one of the great overlooked treasures of global writing.

KAZI ANIS AHMED
Publisher, Bengal Lights Books
Founder, Dhaka Translation Center

The Mercenary

ONE

"The army is here." Azhar Mandal returned with the news. June had just arrived. It rained frequently, pouring hard one moment and disappearing the next. Azhar Mandal had braved the downpour to visit the *ganj*, the market town. If he hadn't had an urgent errand to run, the rain would have stopped him from venturing out. Not to mention the fear of the army. To be honest, none of them had actually seen any army personnel themselves. But they had heard many stories about them. They had also heard many heart-stopping sounds which were proof that the army was indeed close by.

Azhar Mandal had now observed the selfsame army with his very own eyes. It happened quite abruptly; he had had no time to prepare himself. Suddenly, right in front of him, there they were—the army. He had begun to tremble. Nevertheless, he had also found the smart

uniforms, the firearms and the personalities of the soldiers worthy of admiration. His errand remained incomplete. He had gone to the *ganj* to buy some necessary items. But because of the presence of the army many shops hadn't even opened for business. People also appeared to be apathetic, as if no one could recognise anybody else. Not that Azhar Mandal was vexed about it anymore. He was thinking of himself as the lucky man who had seen the army with his own eyes before anyone else from his village had had that opportunity.

As soon as he returned to the village, he announced the arrival of the military with a sombre expression. Because he had seen them with his very own eyes, his description was unending. As he sat on the stoop of Akmal Pradhan's house, he constructed quite a saga. The only claim he didn't make was that the soldiers had four arms each.

The villagers were very curious. They were anxious too, but the anxiety they could keep tamped down for the moment.

Old Bodi was known throughout the village for being crazy. He kept grabbing Azhar Mandal's elbow. But did Azhar Mandal have time to pay attention to this madman? He kept shifting his elbow and continued with his juicy and lengthy description meant for the other members of his audience. Finally, Crazy Bodi lost his temper. He almost twisted Azhar's elbow and said, "Why, you bastard, can't you hear me?"

Azhar Mandal, also enraged, glared at Crazy Bodi. Then he returned his gaze to his audience with a knowing smile, as if to say, what can one do with crazies like that! Still, he didn't completely disappoint Crazy Bodi. He said smugly, "Alright, you loon, what do you want to ask?"

"I want to know—what do the military eat?"

"They eat your shit."

The audience was entertained by both Crazy Bodi's question and Azhar Mandal's answer. They laughed and looked at one another. But Crazy Bodi's feelings were hurt. He said, "Damned backstabber," and grew silent. Their exchange, however, was immediately forgotten as a young man asked Azhar Mandal in a mocking tone, "So, Mandal, did the military inform you of their future plans, like when they're going to visit this area?"

This young man could not be silenced with a judicious retort. Young men like this one were typically quite disrespectful. Who knew what his comeback would be? He might embarrass Azhar Mandal in front of everyone. So Azhar Mandal merely laughed and said, "Oh, they'll be here soon enough, you'll see."

"You're not making that up, are you?"

Azhar Mandal was furious. "What? What did you say?"

"Nothing much. I'm just asking whether you made that up."

"You'll see for yourself. You don't understand yet."

"How am I supposed to understand? Since you haven't shit yourself yet."

Azhar Mandal was apoplectic with rage. Especially when Crazy Bodi began cackling. But there wasn't much he could do. He glared at the young man. It didn't seem to have any effect. So he muttered to himself, "Backstabber! Bastard!" He had every right to be angry at every single one of them. He had brought home such news and here they were, making fun of him.

This wasn't completely true though. Those who were there were actually quite worried. Although they were laughing at the bickering, the laughter was short-lived. The villagers were worried, but they weren't surprised. They had known the army was coming. The news from Dhaka had reached a while ago. Many had been killed in the city, houses had been razed—they knew all that. Those who followed the news had talked about the army spreading out all across the country; they weren't active in just Dhaka anymore. So they were bound to show up in this area one day or another.

What they didn't know was why the military was coming to their village. All the disturbances had taken place in the city. The villagers had, to be honest, participated in a few meetings and rallies when the local leader had visited from the *ganj*. That was expected. However, during the last three months, the *ganj* leader had been conspicuous by his absence. And the one man in the village who was most excited about such things seemed to have disappeared for the last two weeks. Yes, Hares Master had disappeared without telling anyone. Those who followed the news said that Hares Master had left to fight the military.

Along with Hares Master, a few other young men had disappeared from this village as well as the neighbouring villages. Supposedly they were headed for the neighbouring country, India, where they would be trained to fight. Then they were going to destroy the Pakistani army.

Akmal Pradhan protested this claim. His voice heavy with anger, he said, "What are you saying? What, you think it's like taking candy from a baby? They'll just catch the military and finish them off? Don't listen to this rubbish. I'm telling you, Hares Master did not do a good thing. Now the army will arrive and burn down our village."

Akmal Pradhan could not be disbelieved. Although his influence had lessened somewhat in the past year or so, the villagers knew quite well what he was still capable of. Even though some young squirts who used to hang out with Hares Master and the leader from the *ganj* had begun talking against Akmal Pradhan, he was still someone to be reckoned with. Also, Akmal Pradhan was still the one who helped out with loans and advice when someone was in trouble. And then there was Ramjan Sheikh. Many villagers trusted him as well. So now, in these dangerous times, Akmal Pradhan and Ramjan Sheikh were the ones to rely on.

If the military did torch the village, as Akmal Pradhan was predicting, then that did mean danger. But who could save them? After the election they had thought peace was just around the corner. That's what the leader who had visited from the *ganj* for meetings and rallies had told them. What was all this then? Hares Master had said a while ago that the signs were all bad—there was no show of goodwill on the part of the westerners. That was fine; but for the lack of goodwill to manifest itself with such ferocity! When they thought of Hares Master's words, they realised Akmal Pradhan was right. If the army arrived and found out that men from this very village had run off to join the fight against them, it would be doomsday for sure.

Ramjan Sheikh was trying to keep everyone calm. He had promised to save the village from the army, by any means necessary.

A few people were truly relieved. Recent times had shown that Ramjan Sheikh wielded some power too. If Akmal Pradhan did nothing, then surely Ramjan Sheikh would. The majority of villagers were uncertain, however, as to who would be proved right.

Even now, after hearing Azhar Mandal's army-spotting saga, they couldn't quite decide. The brief episodes with Crazy Bodi and that young squirt had not shut Mandal up. He was still going on and on with his description of the military. People ignored the rain and listened to him. It was clear: if the army had reached the *ganj*, they would show up at the village. Since the army had almost arrived, they ought to prepare. Akmal Pradhan's followers looked towards him eagerly.

Akmal Pradhan had been indoors earlier. He had come out to his stoop a little while ago to listen to Azhar Mandal narrate the whole event. He looked worried. In truth, he couldn't figure out what was going to happen next. He didn't know what to tell the villagers. But whether he knew what to say or not, his followers were waiting. Among those waiting to hear from him, there might even be a few from his enemy Ramjan Sheikh's camp. There was no way he was about to confess his ignorance. He should say something. Akmal Pradhan said, "This is worrying news. Do you all understand?"

Everyone already knew that. In the meantime, many more villagers had gathered in front of Akmal Pradhan's house. Both excitement and dismay were growing in the crowd. His fear was that the crowd might just take off towards Ramjan Sheikh's house. That would be a disaster. Akmal Pradhan knew quite well that sometimes authority slipped away through small incidents like this. He could never allow a moment, where power would slip from his hands to Ramjan Sheikh's, to arise. He said, "I have only one thing to say." The crowd looked at him eagerly. Akmal Pradhan paused. Then he almost shouted, "Where is Hares Master now? Where is he?"

The villagers were not prepared for this question. How were they supposed to know where Hares Master was? Some of them did actually know, or perhaps they all knew from hearing and talking about it. But what did it matter? If Hares Master were here, would that have saved them from this peril? A murmur spread across the crowd. That didn't stop Akmal Pradhan's roar. "You tell me, where has Hares Master gone?"

The villagers exchanged glances. The eldest villager present said, "What do we care where Hares Master is? We have nothing to do with Master."

Akmal Pradhan smiled thinly. "*Now* you're saying you have nothing to do with Master. Didn't you attend all those meetings and rallies because Master told you to?"

Many of them had certainly done just that. But bringing all this up now merely threw them into further danger. They had not come here to listen to this. They felt annoyed and impatient. Akmal Pradhan understood but he had no choice. He knew that a speech which lacked an introduction lacked power. He retained his thin smile and said, "Why is the military here? You tell me, why is the military coming to the village? I know why they're coming."

Akmal Pradhan didn't open up about why he thought the army was coming. Instead he asked, "Do you all have our flag in your homes?"

"Our flag" meant the Pakistani flag. Not everybody owned one, since there was never any need to keep a national flag at home. In fact, a few still harboured the flag of Bangladesh in their houses. They had bought them from the *ganj* marketplace and displayed them on a whim. True, they had not flown those flags since March, but they had kept them instead of destroying them. Akmal Pradhan knew all of this quite well. He looked at the silent crowd and roared, "Well? Why don't you say something?"

The elderly man said, "Why are you asking us this? Where are we going to get flags from?" Akmal Pradhan laughed. "Where did you get those Joy Bangla flags from?" There was no answer to that. Akmal Pradhan didn't overdo it. He told everyone who had a Bangladeshi flag to go home and burn it. He instructed those who owned Pakistani flags to display them. He himself kept several flags, of different dimensions, in his house. He told the gathered villagers he wasn't going to bring them out right now. However, for the past two months, members of his household had kept at least one of those flags flying. That flag was already discoloured from the rain and the sun. Akmal Pradhan was aware that he would have to replace it before the army arrived in the village.

He sent two men to summon the imam of the local mosque and the assistant headmaster of the primary school to his house. Now that the army had arrived, there was bound to be some trouble here and there; however, all of that could be managed. They should organise a *dua* at the mosque for the occasion. All the villagers should participate. He was going to assign the assistant headmaster with a responsibility. It would have been better if the headmaster were here. But the headmaster wasn't a local man. Back in March, he had travelled to his own village with his family to spend the vacation. There had been no word from him since then. Even if the headmaster wasn't here, Akmal Pradhan would make do with the assistant headmaster. He would instruct the assistant headmaster to prepare all the students. If necessary, when the army arrived, he would have the boys march with Pakistani flags. And, of course, they would sing the national anthem. But Akmal Pradhan was worried: did all the students know how to sing the Pakistani national anthem?

He felt angry with Hares Master. He felt that somehow or other it was Hares Master's fault that the students didn't know the national anthem, that all the village households didn't possess a Pakistani flag. Before learning anything else, one should learn the national anthem. It made no difference if one learned nothing else. He was realising in his bones right now how important it was for students to learn the national anthem. And everyone should keep a flag at home. It didn't matter if the house had no rice, or no cooking oil. But to not have a flag, that made a difference. For instance, if they had been able to fly a Pakistani flag right now from every house in the village, how happy that would make the army when they arrived!

But that was not to be. He hadn't even been able to fly the Pakistani flag on March 23 because of that Hares Master. This sorrow he would never forget. It had been humiliating. He had served the nation for so long, never had anything like this happened. Now if the army found out that the Pakistani flag had not been flown in this village on March 23, wouldn't he be blamed? Of course, this bit of news wouldn't reach the army's ears unaided. But there was no lack of people in this village—or the next— eager to pour words into the army's ears. There were many who couldn't stand the fact that he wanted what was good for Pakistan, that he wanted to serve Islam. These days, some even taunted him. For instance, Hares Master used to laugh at him, although he wasn't like that before. In fact, when he was younger, Hares Master used to be quite polite. He was lowborn, so Akmal Pradhan had not interacted with him much. But their village wasn't particularly large, so everything happened in full view of everyone. Hares Master changed, gradually, right in front of everyone's eyes. Akmal Pradhan couldn't quite understand what it was that Hares Master wanted. Akmal Pradhan knew quite well—all that talk about liberation, freeing the East Pakistanis from West Pakistani oppression—it was all hogwash. He thought, deep down, Hares Master just wanted to be the *matbar*, the head of the village. The thought made Akmal Pradhan feel astonishment and anger all over again.

He should have finished off Hares Master at the very beginning. But how could he have done that? What did Hares Master have that he could destroy? If there had been anything to destroy he would have handed that responsibility to Kobej a long time ago. That was easy. Just instruct Kobej at the right time. Kobej set fire to houses, slashed the harvest from fields, hacked off heads. He had felt no need to order any of these in the case of Hares Master. All Hares had was his head, and Kobej could chop that off at any moment.

But things had changed drastically over the past couple of years. Hares Master had become cocksure. He didn't want to listen to Akmal Pradhan and laughed off whatever he said. He gathered the young men of the village around him and they all whispered together. All of these were bad signs. The admiration that the young held for Hares Master was something to be afraid of. Hares Master had never insulted him, but the way he talked, his behaviour over the past two years had been a little humiliating for Akmal Pradhan. He could have ordered Kobej to hack his head off. However, there were a few things to be concerned about: Hares was friendly with many people in the *ganj*, and there were even political leaders among them. Beheading him might have caused an uproar. Although money could silence all uproars. Or perhaps Kobej would have carried out his job with such perfection that neither Master's body nor his head would ever be found. But that had never happened.

Akmal Pradhan had been regretting this deeply ever since Hares Master's departure after March. The event on March 23 hadn't been too long ago. It was fresh and vivid in his memory. On the morning of March 23, he had decided to raise the Pakistani flag in the school grounds. Those young upstarts had been flying the Joy Bangla flag everywhere for the past few weeks. A joke, it was all just a joke. You ignorant fools, you neither knew nor understood any of what was happening in Dhaka city, and yet here you were jumping up and down. If you could make sure that once this Joy Bangla flag was raised, you'd never have to take it down, well, that would have been a show of power. But what happened? No, the army used up two bullets in Dhaka, and everything went quiet. All those Joy Bangla flags raised skywards disappeared right away.

Akmal Pradhan had known this was going to happen. So he had felt no pull towards the Joy Bangla flag from the very beginning. If it had seemed like the Joy Bangla flag was here to stay, he would certainly have felt attracted. Anyway, when he tried to raise the Pakistani flag in the school grounds on the morning of March 23, Hares Master had stopped him.

"I *will* hoist the Pakistani flag in this school." Akmal Pradhan had said in anger.

Before Hares Master could respond, a young boy from his group had said, "We *will* stuff that Pakistani flag into a dog's asshole."

Akmal Pradhan glared at the boy, willing him to turn into ashes. That didn't happen, but he didn't abandon his desire to fly the Pakistani flag. He had a group of supporters with him as well. But the young men in Hares Master's group were more eager and energetic. It was their enthusiasm and energy that finally forced him to leave. He stood silently and watched Hares Master raise the Joy Bangla flag. He felt hurt. It was painful that he had failed to raise the Pakistani flag. But the real pain was elsewhere: he was present, right there, and yet someone else had raised the flag. It didn't matter that it was the Joy Bangla flag, it was a flag never-theless. If the Pakistani one couldn't be raised, fine, it wouldn't be. But if anyone should be raising a flag, it should be him—that was all he had wanted.

The crowd in front of his house had grown. This made Akmal Pradhan feel better. Yes, things were going back to the way they used to be. When in trouble, people would come to him. He raised his voice. "Go home, all of you. I'm here. We're Muslims, we're Pakistanis. Let the army come; we will tell them there are no Joy Bangla people in this village. Do you all under-stand what I'm saying?"

There was nothing to misunderstand. Akmal Pradhan's words were quite clear. But the villagers were not satisfied. They wanted to hear something more and they wanted assurance that they would be safe. But Akmal Pradhan wasn't amenable to providing anything extra. He knew from experience not to stray too far from his capabilities. Eventually that led to people losing faith. When Akmal Pradhan said no more, the crowd began to disperse. Many sped off towards Ramjan Sheikh's house, anxiety etched on their faces.

Akmal Pradhan realised where they were headed. Angrily, he said, "Where are they going, huh? Where? Was I telling lies all this time that they have to go to someone else?" However, the only ones who heard him were those standing nearby, the people whom he considered loyal and favoured. They laughed. One of them said, "Don't worry about those little shits. When the army arrives, just ask them to whack them on their asses."

Not everyone headed for Ramjan Sheikh's house though. When Akmal Pradhan was done talking, many villagers just went home. One man told others to pack their knickknacks and necessaries. Because they might have to run at any moment. Sometimes the army just wouldn't listen. They torched and looted houses, and abducted women and girls. This had happened in some villages.

As the crowd thinned, Akmal Pradhan grew busy with his own people. The army would surely arrive soon. If not today, tomorrow, or maybe the day after. He had to put together a plan. Suppose the army knew everything about this village. Suppose they knew many villagers had attended meetings and marched in rallies to support Joy Bangla. That leaders had come from the *ganj* to make speeches and, their blood all hot, the villagers had applauded. That even on March 23, the Joy Bangla flag had flown high in this village. Suppose they knew all this.

Hares Master could be blamed for everything. But the question was, would the army believe it? What if they said: Okay, we get it, Hares Master is to blame for everything in this village. We believe what you're telling us. But what were *you* doing then? Tell us, what were you up to? Did you stop him? *Batao*, tell us.

He would respond, of course he had tried to stop Master. But there were just too many of those infidels. So his efforts were mostly futile.

Otherwise he would gladly have put his life on the line for Pakistan. But if he was then asked why he hadn't actually placed his life on the line—that would be a difficult question to answer. Perhaps they wouldn't ask that. Surely they didn't have time to bother with such minor issues!

In the meantime, the mosque's muezzin and the assistant headmaster of the school had showed up. There was no reason to, but he scolded them anyway. He glared at the muezzin and demanded to know why the azan had not been sounded yet.

The muezzin was taken aback. Why would he be calling out the azan at this odd hour? Akmal Pradhan told him that the great army of Pakistan had arrived in the *ganj*. Tomorrow, or the day after, they would reach the village. So the peril had passed. The muezzin should call out the azan to signal to all that the danger was gone. This would raise morale among the villagers. Also, this way those who didn't know yet would learn that the danger was gone. The muezzin listened wide-eyed. Akmal Pradhan told him to go door to door once he had called out the azan. This afternoon at the mosque, there would be a session reciting the holy Quran as well as prayers and blessings. All the villagers should be present there.

When he was done talking, Akmal Pradhan handed the muezzin a flag emblazoned with the sickle moon and star. The muezzin received it with due respect. Pradhan smiled. "I'm entrusting this to you. Go and fly it at the mosque. And listen, tell everyone that I am the one who gave you this flag. If the army asks you, where did you get this flag, tell them my name." The muezzin had no objection. He left for the mosque immediately, carrying the moon-and-star bedecked flag.

Akmal Pradhan now busied himself with the assistant headmaster, shouting at him without hesitation. He said he wanted to have the school boys singing the national anthem of Pakistan within the hour.

This was a difficult task, and the assistant headmaster baulked. Akmal Pradhan silenced him with another scolding. No excuse was acceptable. It was mandatory for the students to know the national anthem. If they didn't, then the teachers were at fault. Because it meant that the teachers had failed to impart knowledge that was urgent. This failure should be enough to cost them their jobs. More importantly, the army was about to arrive. So the students had to learn how to sing the national anthem and how to march 'left right' immediately. The assistant headmaster should also make sure that each student knew how to recite the kalimas. In this, Akmal Pradhan was a little more considerate towards him. He decided that the parents could be tasked with teaching them the kalimas. The assistant headmaster was happy to have his burden lessened somewhat. The worry was that he himself didn't know the national anthem perfectly. How was he supposed to remember a song that was written in a different language, a song which he didn't understand at all? Although he wouldn't have been able to remember it even if it had been in Bangla. He wasn't brave enough to say this to Akmal Pradhan. He knew he would get shouted at. And bastard that he was, Akmal Pradhan might even repeat it to the army when they arrived. What a hassle, where was he supposed to find the national anthem now? It would have been easier if Hares was still around. That man knew everything. There was no need to provide the assistant headmaster with a Pakistani flag. Because even if it was old, the school was supposed to have a Pakistani flag already. Akmal Pradhan himself had gifted the flag to the school a few years ago. It hadn't been used much. It had not been displayed after March. Not that it had been flown much even before March. So it shouldn't look too ratty. It would do. The question was, was the flag still intact? Or had it disappeared? Hares Master hadn't burned it, had he? When he asked, the assistant headmaster reassured him. Yes, the flag was still there, and he would make sure it was raised right away.

Once he had done all these things, Akmal Pradhan felt a little relieved. He didn't know for sure what would happen once the army was actually here. He didn't think anything too bad would happen. Most of it he had taken care of. The rest was just luck. The others present felt the same way. But they were all a little worried about Ramjan Sheikh. Ramjan Sheikh was extremely sly, he had cunning written all over him. If he pulled some trick in the meantime, it could spell disaster. Did his plans contain any gap or loophole that might allow Ramjan Sheikh to pull a trick? Akmal Pradhan considered it and couldn't find anything.

However, sometimes such gaps evaded his notice. He should ask the others. But they couldn't discover any loophole either. Akmal Pradhan turned to Kobej. So far, he had asked Kobej nothing. Kobej was usually like an angry buffalo, but occasionally he would say something smart. Once in a while, he would lay out a plan or give some advice that was surprising. So Akmal Pradhan turned to Kobej.

"Kobej."

Kobej didn't respond.

"Kobej."

Kobej still didn't respond.

Akmal Pradhan grew annoyed. "Hey, Kobej, can't you hear me calling you?"

"I heard." Kobej stretched himself. "I heard. Tell me what you wanted to say."

TWO

Kobej had not seemed remotely worried all this time. He had been sitting on a bench behind Akmal Pradhan, feeling despondent. So many reasons for sadness. Right now, he himself wasn't sure why he was sad. Most of what was being discussed so far had not reached his ears. He had been smoking one bidi after another. At first, he had been entertained by Azhar Mandal's description of the military. But he wasn't particularly interested in the army. He had seen them before. He knew that they only had two arms and two legs. They did, however, know how to use guns.

He had nothing to do now. He wouldn't have been sitting on Akmal Pradhan's stoop all this time if that had not been the case. But he had nothing to do and nowhere to go. So he sat behind Akmal Pradhan, staring at the gathered crowd, or as far as his eyes could see in the distance. At times, he had lost his temper. His temper gave him a lot of trouble. Sometimes it twisted so that he couldn't control it.

For instance, minutes earlier, for no apparent reason, he had felt the need to slap Azhar Mandal. Then he had wanted to shake him by the hair and level a kick on his buttocks that would drop him to the ground. He had grown angry, extremely angry. It wasn't just Azhar Mandal; his anger was focussed on various people in the crowd. He wanted to invite someone to sit beside him, and then grab them by the throat.

Such anger was not good. Kobej knew this. It was dangerous when temper took control of a person. Kobej had seen that he got into some kind of trouble every time his anger took over his head. Akmal Pradhan had told him many times that his hotheadedness would be the end of him. But what could he do? It wasn't as if he willed himself to lose his temper. It just happened. He had tried to control himself in different ways. He rarely spoke to people. He didn't pay attention to everything that went on around him. Like right now, when his anger raised its head as he listened to Azhar Mandal's military saga, he focussed on something else. He paid no attention to what people were saying, or even to Akmal Pradhan's grand speech. However, it wasn't possible to block everything out completely. So he had heard some of it; some of it had reached his ears. He had never liked too much discussion. What was the point of all this talk? He had never seen the need for it, and it irritated him.

When Akmal Pradhan called him by name, he didn't want to respond. However, if Akmal Pradhan called, you answered. So he responded the third time, saying, "I heard."

"If you heard why don't you say something?" Akmal Pradhan sounded angry.

There was no answer to that one, so Kobej kept quiet.

"Son, tell me one thing for real."

"I see you're just twisting your words—you're not actually saying anything."

"Don't be like that. Why is there no smile on your face?"

"I'm fine. Just tell me what you want to say."

"Will we be able to take care of the situation if the military do come?"

"How am I supposed to know?" Kobej was genuinely surprised.

"You'll give that Ramjan Sheikh hell, won't you?"

"Oh, that!" Kobej laughed. "That's what you're getting at?"

"If not you, who am I supposed to ask?"

"What am I supposed to do?"

"Give him hell. Give that son-of-a-bitch hell."

Kobej laughed again. "Instead of telling me, you should say that to the military when they come."

"I will. But right now, use your head, my boy. Come up with a plan."

"When the military comes, don't let him go near them."

"How will I stop him? He will try to get near them for sure."

"Then I can't tell you anything else right now. My head is on fire."

There was no point asking Kobej anything when his head was on fire. Disappointed, Akmal Pradhan turned to the others. "You lot, go home. Go and pray to Allah."

It took a while for everyone to get going. They talked a little longer with Akmal Pradhan about other matters. Then, one by one, they said goodbye. A few of them had wanted to eat before they left. It would save some food in their households if they could eat a meal here. Also, the food cooked in this house tasted better, not to mention that there were usually several courses. But Akmal Pradhan's expression made it very clear that this wasn't likely. So they left as well. Kobej had lit another bidi in the meantime. Akmal Pradhan asked him in a heavy voice, "Kobej, why did you insult me like that?"

"When did I insult you?"

"You did. Now tell me what's bothering you. You look as if a monkey took a shit in your mouth."

Kobej was silent. There was no answer to the question of what was bothering him.

"Do you have no work?" Akmal Pradhan smiled slightly as he asked.

This was true. When Kobej was on a job he had no time to be grumpy. But the way things were right now, there was no work to be found in the village. There was also no chance that he would get a call for a job from a nearby village or the *ganj*.

Kobej had broken out of prison around mid-March. It couldn't exactly be called a jailbreak. Because no one had really tried to stop them when they made a run for it. Kobej had found it amusing. He had had to go to the police station or jail several times before this. But there was no question of breaking out on those occasions. There had been no need to, either. Most times the issue was somehow settled after he made several visits to the police station. Only once had he had to spend a whole year in prison.

This time the jailbreak was quite well-planned. A few educated prisoners even gave speeches over several days. Kobej didn't understand most of it. Like everyone else, however, he was very enthusiastic about breaking out. It was when he was out that things got tricky. There were rallies and marches and meetings everywhere. Everywhere. He wasn't interested in them though. He wanted to get back to his village. But he had no money.

His village was quite far from the town where he had been imprisoned. He would have to take the train. He wasn't worried about the train fare. Who could make him pay against his will? But he would need to feed himself on the way. He hated everything when he was hungry. Then he discovered that another man who had broken out with him was in a similar bind. They joined forces and took the opportunity to carry out a little looting here and there. They got enough to last a few days. Kobej was very angry with the police at that time. They were the cause of all his troubles. If they had just locked him up in the prison at the *ganj*, he wouldn't have had to go to all this trouble. But no, as soon as they caught him, they had to transfer him straight to the *sadar* town because "times were bad." The police station didn't have enough space, so they sent him to prison. Now he was a criminal. His case hadn't been heard by the court yet. Kobej thought it would be better for him if the court heard his case as soon as possible. Akmal Pradhan had assured him of that.

Because if the court heard the case, it would be settled very quickly. There were no witnesses against him. So no allegation would stick. But now this thorn in his side would remain. Now the police would be looking for Kobej again. The case would be reopened. All of this was a hassle, a waste of time.

Kobej spent a few days with his friend-in-need. Finally the man said, "My friend, now you head your way, and I'll head mine. If we get caught, those sons-of-bitches will just lock us up again."

There was no chance of them being caught though. Even if they wanted to surrender, there was no one around to lock them up. Still, they headed towards their destinations. Kobej reached his village on the morning of the twenty-fifth. He had been a little confused as to whether he should head straight for the village. Maybe he'd arrive to find out that the police had already come looking for him. But where else could he have gone? Anyway, Akmal Pradhan was there. He would be able to advise him as needed.

Akmal Pradhan was quite surprised when he saw him. "Kobej, you?"

"Yes, it's me." Kobej chuckled.

"Where did you come from? They let you out?"

Kobej laughed again. "Yeah, they let me go. I'm free."

"Why?" There was doubt in Akmal Pradhan's voice.

Kobej told him the whole story, in complete detail. Akmal Pradhan instructed him to remain in hiding for a few days. It was no big deal to hide in his own village. He could spend days at a time in one of the rooms of Pradhan's enormous household. The next day was March

26. The apocalypse unleashed didn't touch them, safe as they were in their village. But they heard many things. Akmal Pradhan realised, as did Kobej, there was no longer any need for him to stay in hiding.

Since then he had just been sitting around. All he had to do was eat, sleep, smoke bidis and keep company with Akmal Pradhan. In the meantime, Pradhan had made a proposition which Kobej had been mulling over for the past month. Yes, it was a proposal to kill someone. But Kobej knew there were some snags. There was no rush. He had learned from hard experience that rushing these jobs meant messing them up. Like last time: haste was what led to him being caught. It still made him unhappy. It was just one killing, a single murder, why did he get caught trying to pull it off? Why wasn't he able to pull it off with no impediments, no witnesses? Whenever he thought of his last job, he felt ashamed. Akmal Pradhan had abused him roundly at the time. "You idiot! Kobej, you've behaved like a fool!"

Akmal Pradhan's invectives were justified. Because the murder had been on his account. Kobej had realised his mistake as soon as he had committed it. But he hadn't wanted to admit it. So he told Akmal Pradhan straight up, "Whether I've been stupid or not, I was supposed to kill someone, and I have."

"Now you'll get caught. I'm telling you, you'll get caught."

Kobej had blown off Akmal Pradhan's fear. "Right. Just because you say so. No one can catch me."

Of course, he *had* been caught. Akmal Pradhan tried his best but couldn't get him released. But Kobej had not divulged any information to the police. He knew that there would be no trouble even if the case went to court, because no one would dare give evidence against him. Many people had seen him—he had killed the man right in the middle of a marketplace, there must have been many witnesses. But out of sheer self-interest, they wouldn't come near the court. If anyone did decide to bear witness, Akmal Pradhan would take care of it. But before the case ever reached the courtroom, they broke out of jail and March 26 happened.

Right now, he wasn't worried about his last murder. It might be a problem in the future. Unless Akmal Pradhan somehow managed to make it go away in the meantime. Once something was documented in a police station it was difficult to alter. Although there were other ways. Like, maybe the perpetrator would be right in front of everyone's eyes, but the police could never actually find him. Unless someone raised a ruckus, or created some pressure, why would the police be bothered to catch them anyway? Akmal Pradhan could probably organise something like that. But that could wait. Right now Kobej was in no mood to become embroiled in fresh trouble.

Akmal Pradhan's stoop had almost emptied out. Pradhan turned to Kobej. "Come on, let's go indoors." Not everyone had access to the inner quarters of Pradhan's house, but Kobej did. Not by himself though, only if Akmal Pradhan was with him. His chamber in the inner house was large and held quite a few luxuries. Once inside, Pradhan settled himself on his bed, while Kobej sat on a stool beside him. Tea and snacks had been ordered. He had decided that after they had had some tea and eaten something, he was going to make the rounds of the village with Kobej in tow.

Kobej had no such inclination. He had guessed Pradhan's plans and was fidgeting. Making the rounds with Pradhan was annoying. He would stop here for a bit, there for a while, chatting first with this person, and then with someone else. It seemed pointless to Kobej. What was the need for so much talk in this one lifetime? He knew actions were more important than talk. But perhaps talking was also important sometimes. Otherwise, why would someone as smart as Akmal Pradhan talk so much? Even if it was important, Kobej didn't like having to think. Going out with Akmal Pradhan would just irritate him even more, so he began looking for a chance to make himself scarce.

But Akmal Pradhan wanted Kobej beside him. When the tea arrived,

Pradhan blew on it loudly. Then he took a long sip, finishing almost half at one go. He looked at Kobej and asked lightly, "So, what did you decide about Ramjan Sheikh, Kobej?"

He'd made the proposal about a month ago. Akmal Pradhan had no need to prevaricate with Kobej. So the proposal had been quite direct—Ramjan Sheikh needed to be eliminated. Even for Kobej, it wasn't an easy job. It was hard, quite hard. The responsibility of getting rid of Ramjan Sheikh brought with it the need to consider many things before and after. Kobej had found out that when thinking of Ramjan Sheikh, his temper remained ice cool. Murder, Kobej knew, was no big deal. It wasn't as if, to him, a killing just meant fistfuls of money. It wasn't just the money, sometimes he simply enjoyed killing someone. Since he enjoyed it, he would probably enjoy killing Ramjan Sheikh as well. Plus, he would get a lot of money for this one. Akmal Pradhan had mentioned a lot of money. But Kobej also knew that it would be hard to manage the repercussions of murdering Ramjan Sheikh. Even Akmal Pradhan might not be able to pull that off. What then? He would lose out from all sides.

Once Akmal Pradhan made his proposal, Kobej had tried to work up a rage against Ramjan Sheikh. This was not particularly difficult.

There were several—quite logical—reasons for him to be angry with Ramjan Sheikh. For instance, Ramjan Sheikh couldn't stand Kobej. This was very clear from the way he spoke to Kobej. As if Kobej was an insect rather than a human being. This would have been enough. He could just get himself to be angry about this and finish Ramjan Sheikh off. But Kobej had found out that while it was possible to be enraged with Ramjan Sheikh, as soon as he started thinking of killing him, he cooled down. His anger dissipated.

This, Kobej had figured, was a good thing all around. It was true that he couldn't take the same approach to Ramjan Sheikh as he would with any run-of-the-mill person. That was the thing—it was all very well to commit the murder, but how would he manage the fallout? Akmal Pradhan was sometimes too quick when rushing into such things. Ever since he had proposed this to Kobej, he had been hustling him twice a day. Each time proffering the lure of payment. The amount of money on offer was steadily increasing. Kobej knew it would grow further. In fact, he knew that if he demanded double the amount overnight, Akmal Pradhan would not demur. But Kobej was not thinking of money right now. Money was an issue, it would always be an issue. But right now he was thinking he was not going to rush the Ramjan Sheikh job in any way.

If Akmal Pradhan hadn't been so anxious about Ramjan Sheikh he would have guessed by now that Kobej was suffering doubts over the business. Kobej would never, however, volunteer this information. Never let anyone see vulnerability. Not even those closest to you. They immediately began thinking of you as a coward. They were no longer able to rely on you. You lost value. So he couldn't tell anyone about his indecisiveness. He had to keep that bottled in.

But Kobej also realised he had to prepare himself. Alongside Akmal Pradhan's pressure, another thing was unsettling him. Akmal Pradhan was afraid that the way things were going, Ramjan Sheikh's influence would soon eclipse his. Villagers would go to Ramjan Sheikh in their times of trouble, and listen to what he had to say. No one would come to Akmal Pradhan. If no one came to Akmal Pradhan, would there be any need for Kobej anymore? This was what Kobej was afraid of. Right now he took on jobs for Akmal Pradhan; this was enough to clothe and feed him. But what if it turned out that Ramjan Sheikh would decide what jobs needed to be carried out, and Akmal Pradhan no longer had any say? Kobej would have no work. Which meant he would starve. He had no other skills. He owned no land. So if Akmal Pradhan's power to give him work was compromised, dark days were ahead for him. It wasn't as if Ramjan Sheikh would call on him. No, that was something Ramjan Sheikh wouldn't do. Because Ramjan Sheikh had Idris to carry out his jobs. Idris already threw Kobej some looks sometimes! If Ramjan Sheikh surpassed Akmal Pradhan one day, Idris would most certainly try to knock off Kobej. He realised Ramjan Sheikh needed to be killed in his own interest. Kobej finished his tea and lit another bidi.

Akmal Pradhan had strong objections to Kobej's choice of tobacco. He couldn't tolerate the smell of bidis. He himself smoked proper tobacco. He had told Kobej to at least switch to cigarettes. But Kobej was adamant. Cigarettes didn't do it for him.

When he lit his bidi, Akmal Pradhan wrinkled his nose and glanced at him. Then he stood up and looked himself over. He turned to Kobej and said, "Come, Kobej, let's go."

"Go where?"

"Let's walk around the village."

For a second Kobej thought of saying he didn't feel like it, of asking what he would get out of making the rounds, other than aching feet? But he didn't. Doing the rounds with Akmal Pradhan was part of his job. Besides, he needed to get some money from Akmal Pradhan today. His pockets were empty. He didn't have enough to even buy another pack of bidis.

Akmal Pradhan changed his skullcap before they left. He looked Kobej over and then held out another one to him. "Take this."

"Why are you giving me a skullcap?" Kobej asked in surprise.

"Why am I giving you a skullcap? What do people do with caps?"

"They wear them on their heads."

"So you wear one on your head too."

"Do you think I'm mad?"

Akmal Pradhan was incensed. He scolded Kobej for talking like an infidel. "*Shala*, you *are* mad. Saying whatever comes to mind."

"If I go out wearing a skullcap people will think I'm mad for sure."

Akmal Pradhan insisted.

"Why are you forcing me?" Kobej was annoyed. "Tell me why I should put this cap on my head."

Akmal Pradhan was irked. "You bastard, the military's coming."

"If they're coming, they're coming. What's that got to do with me?"

"What's that got to do with you?" Akmal Pradhan looked at him goggle-eyed. "You bastard, the military will shove a bamboo right up your arse and keep you standing straight."

"So if I wear a skullcap, they won't shove this bamboo up my arse?" Kobej asked solemnly.

"No, they won't." Akmal Pradhan informed him with equal solemnity.

"Why won't they?"

"If you wear this skullcap it means you're a Muslim."

Kobej stared at Akmal Pradhan for a few moments and began laughing.

"Why are you laughing?" Akmal Pradhan grew angry.

"No reason, I just felt like laughing." Kobej laughed as he replied. "Okay, give me that cap, let me put it on!" With the skullcap settled on his scalp, Kobej set out with Akmal Pradhan. Pradhan headed for the school first. He was furious when he didn't find anyone there. He turned to Kobej and said, "What did I tell that fool of a teacher, and what has he done instead?"

Kobej assured him. "He's going around the houses getting the boys together."

"Who told you that?"

"No one told me. I just know."

Pradhan glared at Kobej for a few moments. Then gradually he seemed to feel reassured. He brightened up and finally asked Kobej what he thought of his plan. Kobej laughed. "Why ask me? I don't understand these things."

"Why?" Akmal Pradhan was a little disappointed at Kobej's stupidity. "What don't you understand? Shouldn't school students know a thing like the national anthem?"

"They should know it because the army is coming?"

"You're just twisting my words, Kobej. Yes, that's why they should know it."

"Are the military men all teachers? Are they going to test the students?"

Akmal Pradhan looked at Kobej again. "You're an idiot. Listen, you son of a bitch, the army is the teacher of teachers." He explained the way things were to Kobej in detail. Pakistani citizens should, of course, know the national anthem. Students, especially, should know it. They should also know the kalimas. If they didn't know the kalimas they weren't Muslims. And if they weren't Muslims, they weren't Pakistanis. They were kafirs, infidels. The army might arrive and quiz the students on the national anthem or the kalimas. If they had already learned it by then, the military would be very happy.

Kobej nodded frequently as he listened to Akmal Pradhan. Then, in an easy voice, he asked, "Weren't the students of this village Pakistanis or Muslims all this time?"

Akmal Pradhan's brow creased. "Why do you ask that?"

Kobej smiled and said it was Akmal Pradhan who had instructed the assistant headmaster to teach the students the national anthem and the kalimas.

Pradhan nodded. Yes, indeed, he had given such instructions. Kobej laughed again. Then all this time the students had known neither the national anthem nor the kalimas. So they had been neither Pakistanis nor Muslims.

"How do you store such warped ideas in your belly!" Akmal Pradhan reined in his anger. "You don't understand any of this, Kobej."

This was true. Kobej didn't really understand any of this. It was all very strange. He had been watching it unfold ever since his jailbreak. That roar when people chanted "Joy Bangla! Joy Bangla!" What was Joy Bangla? They said liberation was coming. They said the westerners, the Punjabis, had oppressed them these last twenty-four years. That they had looted everything from this land. There was no way to remain one with West Pakistan. Now this land would be liberated. No one would live in sorrow any longer. No one would go hungry. Kobej's response when he had heard this had been: Pooh!

But that was about all he had thought. He hadn't wasted his time pondering on it. What difference did it make to him whether the country was liberated or not? He gained nothing by worrying about it, and in any case, he didn't understand any of it. When he had returned to the village he had heard about the incident involving Hares Master from Akmal Pradhan. It made him very angry. How dare he fly the Joy Bangla flag in the school

compound after Akmal Pradhan had told him not to! How dare
he! If he found Hares anywhere near him he would chop him
into two pieces. But a few days later, he thought about Hares
again and felt surprised. Hares used to be a decent sort, never
poking his nose where it didn't belong. So why did he suddenly,
for no apparent reason, get into a fight with a man like Akmal
Pradhan over flying this Joy Bangla flag?

And now he couldn't understand why everyone had to learn
the national anthem and the kalimas just because the army was
about to arrive. If they had managed to get by all this time without having learned either, why was it suddenly so necessary to
learn them now? Kobej didn't feel he had been at a particular disadvantage all this time because he didn't know these things. Nor
had anyone ever labelled the students kafirs. They seemed to have
been Muslim and Pakistani all along. This was the trouble—all
this Joy Bangla, kalima, Pakistani national anthem—he couldn't
fathom any of it. He didn't want to, either. But sometimes the
whole thing coiled itself into such a knot that he had no choice
but to think about it, and ask someone. The way he had just
asked Akmal Pradhan, because he truly didn't understand what
was going on. Now at least he thought he had got it: it was possible to exist as a Pakistani and a Muslim without knowing the
national anthem and the kalimas. However, if the army were
about to show up, it was best to learn them right away. Kobej
succeeded in getting rid of these thoughts quite soon.

After visiting the school, Akmal Pradhan went to the
mosque. The muezzin had already raised the flag Akmal Pradhan
had given him. Pradhan reminded him: if the army asked where
he had got the flag, he was to name Akmal Pradhan. The muezzin

joyfully nodded his understanding. He was proud to have been able to fly a brand new flag at his mosque. That made Akmal Pradhan happy as well. He asked Kobej, "What do you think of the new flag, Kobej?"

Kobej nodded his approval. Then he asked, "Why did you put the flag here?" Akmal Pradhan was surprised. "Shouldn't there be a flag at the mosque?" Kobej didn't get it. He asked again, why was it a problem if there were no flag here? Akmal Pradhan couldn't quite answer him. It would make the army happy to see the Pakistani flag there. Kobej wanted to know why. This had been a mosque before the flag, and now that the flag was there, it was still a mosque. Akmal Pradhan seemed taken aback. He said the Pakistani flag flying would signal to the army that this was a mosque for Muslims. No sooner had the words escaped his mouth than he realised how silly they sounded. He bit down on his tongue and said, "Shouldn't we make sure the military knows that this mosque belongs to Pakistani people?"

Should they? Perhaps. But a mosque was a mosque, at any given moment. Kobej didn't want to think about this anymore. He followed Akmal Pradhan and kept walking. Pradhan was now visiting one house after another. Kobej had nothing to do but follow him around. Pradhan visited various families and spoke to many people. Kobej didn't pay attention. His mind was back on Ramjan Sheikh.

Akmal Pradhan brought up Ramjan Sheikh again on their way back. Night had descended by then. The rumour about the army had made people quieter than usual. Kobej turned his flashlight on. Akmal Pradhan walked beside him. He looked happy. He was satisfied with his meetings with the village folk. Yes, the villagers were still dependent on him. Everyone had heard that when the army arrived, they tortured people. Pradhan had to save the villagers from such a fate. It would be difficult, but he had to do it. Of course, Pradhan had not promised he would keep every single person safe. He was thinking of things a little differently. He would take this opportunity to eliminate a few insubordinate bodies from the mix, and try to push Ramjan Sheikh into a corner. Although, if he managed to keep the villagers safe from the military, Ramjan Sheikh would be cornered anyway. Tough times ahead, thought Akmal Pradhan as he moved forward. Who knows what would happen? He sighed deeply and said, "Kobej."

"Yes," Kobej responded tersely.

"Have you decided?"

Kobej looked at Pradhan. "I'm referring to Ramjan Sheikh," Akmal Pradhan said in a tired voice.

"I'm thinking," Kobej replied after a pause.

"Thinking what?"

Kobej didn't reply. Akmal Pradhan grew angry. Furious, he mentioned that Kobej's father had been a *lethel*, a stick-fighter for hire, as had been his grandfather. Both had been capable of taking on fifty men singlehandedly. There was not a village where their names were unknown. How could Kobej say something like this—he, the son and grandson of such men? Words like "thinking" didn't suit Kobej, heir to that lineage. Akmal Pradhan's words provoked no reaction in Kobej. He lit his last bidi and said, "I need some money."

"Why? Why do you need money?"

Akmal Pradhan's response made Kobej angry but he managed to suppress it. "You know why I need money. I don't have any."

Pradhan was silent for a few seconds but then he nodded to say he would give Kobej some money.

"I don't even have enough to buy my bidis."

"Shall I give you a thousand taka, Kobej? Will you take it?"

Kobej said nothing for a long time. Then, in a weary voice, he said, "I told you, I'm thinking."

"Thinking, right?"

Kobej nodded. Akmal Pradhan didn't say another word the rest of the way. When they reached home he told Kobej to wait. He went inside to wash up and change his clothes before he emerged again. He expressed regret at missing the hour of the namaz and held out twenty taka to Kobej. Then, facing Kobej, he sat down.

After some moments of silence, he asked if Kobej knew that a war had begun. But before Kobej could respond, he went on to say that the war being waged was between Muslims and infidels. That leader from the *ganj*, Hares Master and all those from this village who had fled with Hares Master—every single one of them was an infidel. There were more infidels like them. They wanted to split Pakistan into two. Once that was done, they would go and shack up with those Hindus in India. This would then become a Hindu country.

But Akmal Pradhan was rooting for Pakistan. He said, "My life for Pakistan." Because they couldn't allow those Hindus to take over this land. What would they answer to Allah in the Great Assembly, the field of Hashar? This war was Muslims against infidels. Kobej knew a little bit about these issues; he had heard people talk. He nodded frequently as Akmal Pradhan spoke. This encouraged Pradhan. He took a little break but went on to say that Ramjan Sheikh was sort of on Pakistan's side. At least, that's what he told people. He claimed to be a Muslim. Nevertheless, now that Muslims were at war against infidels, Kobej could seize the opportunity if he wanted to.

What opportunity? Akmal Pradhan informed Kobej that he could take this chance to eliminate Ramjan Sheikh. He smiled and gazed at Kobej.

"You're saying people will think the infidels killed Ramjan Sheikh?" Kobej asked.

Akmal Pradhan nodded vigorously. "Of course they will. Why wouldn't they?"

"You're talking of *mukti*, the freedom fighters?"

"The *mukti bahini*?" Akmal Pradhan was a little surprised. "Who told you about them?"

"No one," Kobej said. "I'm just hearing about them from people."

Pradhan agreed: yes, people were indeed calling the infidels *mukti*.

But these *mukti*, these freedom fighters, were the ones trying to kill those who were in favour of Pakistan. If Kobej finished off Ramjan Sheikh, people would just assume the *mukti* had killed him. Because the *mukti* would come after supporters of Pakistan.

"The things you say!" Kobej laughed. "Then the *mukti* could come after you too."

Akmal Pradhan was taken aback at first, but then he broke into laughter. Sure, they could come after him. But he would never give those infidels that chance. Anyway, how long could the kafirs go on? Victory would come to the Muslims, or those who were supporting Pakistan. After all, they had both Allah and the army on their side. The military would beat everyone into submission in two days. There was no way those infidels could take over as long as the army was here. Akmal Pradhan was siding with the military, so it wouldn't be easy for anyone to just walk in and kill him. That was an easy calculation.

Kobej laughed and said he didn't understand all these calculations.

That made Akmal Pradhan happy. He slapped Kobej on the back. If he didn't understand, he shouldn't bother. What was the point of trying to understand everything anyway? The only thing to be said was that now that there was an opportunity, Kobej shouldn't delay on the issue of Ramjan Sheikh. He should finish the job before the military came in and beat everyone to a pulp.

"I'll give you a thousand taka, my boy." Akmal Pradhan ended his little speech with an offer.

"Why do you keep bringing up money? I told you, I'm thinking it over."

Kobej's response didn't deflate Akmal Pradhan. It did, however, keep him quiet for a while. Then he said, "Kobej, do you want some land?"

"Land! You're talking of land!" Kobej was surprised.

"Yes, I'm talking of land."

Kobej was silent.

"Where do you want it? Just tell me and I'll write it over to you."

"You want to tie me down with land?"

Akmal Pradhan protested at Kobej's question. No, no, that's not how he was thinking at all. It didn't suit Kobej to be tied down by land, to be farming like an ordinary person! Pradhan knew that quite well. But everyone needed a bit of land. A piece of earth beneath their feet. It would be useful in times ahead. If he started accruing land now, it would be enormously useful for Kobej in the future. And he too had need for a household, a family. If not today, then tomorrow. Or maybe the day after.

Kobej thought about it when he was in bed that night. It was raining again. Although it was only early June, it was already a little chilly. Kobej couldn't fall asleep. One thousand taka was a lot of money if he got it in hand all at once. Akmal Pradhan would probably give it to him at one go; he might even increase the amount if asked.

And why only cash! Akmal Pradhan had promised to write over some land to him. Land was, of course, an evil thing. No one knew this better than Kobej. He knew all about the fights and the murders that revolved around land ownership. But it was also true that everyone needed a little bit of land. Yes, a piece of earth all one's own, beneath one's feet. It seemed like a dream.

These days, once in a while, his heart wanted to settle down somewhere. The bigger issue was that he would have money in his pockets only as long as Akmal Pradhan had work to be done. At least Akmal Pradhan paid him whenever he asked, even without work. But those payments had no urgency to them. Pradhan paid unwillingly, Kobej knew that. Now if he had a piece of land, even if he didn't cultivate it himself, he could get someone else to do the farming. That might mean a regular source of income. So he should say yes to Akmal Pradhan's proposal. His heart wanted to say yes.

But killing Ramjan Sheikh would be a tough proposition. He was no less powerful than Akmal Pradhan. Kobej understood that quite well. If Sheikh's people figured out that Kobej was the one who had done it, they would exact their revenge. But, Kobej wondered, how much power would Ramjan Sheikh's men have after his death? Just as he, himself—Kobej was quite clear—would have no power at all if Akmal Pradhan was gone. The same should hold true for Ramjan Sheikh's men in his absence.

There was an additional benefit awaiting him though. Akmal Pradhan was right. He could do the job and shift the blame to those infidels, the ones whom people were calling the *mukti bahini*. He was hearing about the *mukti bahini* more and more, even from ordinary villagers. In some areas they were fighting against the army and those who stood in favour of Pakistan. Let them—Kobej was not about to tax his brains over them.

But, Kobej pondered, if the *mukti bahini* arrived in the village in the wake of the military, it would make his job easier. Yes, they certainly would, he thought. If the military had reached the *ganj*, they would show up here. And if the *mukti bahini* sniffed them out and followed them to the village, his calculations would be proved right. He could hack off Ramjan Sheikh's head. He was delighted with this train of thought. But he did want to think it over a little more.

Those Pakistan–Muslim–Joy Bangla–Bangladesh issues still remained. He understood none of it and felt no curiosity either. This, he understood: if Ramjan Sheikh was not clearly on the side of Pakistan, it would be hard to convince people that he had been killed by *mukti*. Would Ramjan Sheikh support Pakistan openly? Probably, Kobej thought. That was what Akmal Pradhan was predicting. A few days ago, he had witnessed Ramjan Sheikh throwing his weight around. Sheikh had been pronouncing that everyone who had left with Hares Master, as well as those who would leave from now on, would have their homes torched. Kobej's face was slowly suffused by a broad smile. He began to feel drowsy. In his half-sleep, Kobej's little slice of land kept growing and growing.

THREE

The Pakistani army reached the village the following afternoon. The news spread fast once they were spotted at the edge of the village and the dull roar of their vehicles reached people's ears. People shuttered their doors and windows. The Pakistani army didn't shoot a single bullet, nor did they yell or scream. But the whole village turned cool and quiet, like a yard freshly layered with clay.

The army troop set up camp in the large field in front of the primary school, securing their temporary accommodation against attacks in a very short period of time. Some people watched the scene through the gaps in their fences, or through windows opened a crack. But no one was brave enough to approach them.

The troop itself looked as if it was in no hurry. As if the men had just returned to a place long familiar. As if they were weary from their long journey back. As if they were resting awhile before venturing out to say hello to everyone.

Their silence and their lack of urgency confused the villagers. A few villagers brightened, thinking nothing much would happen. A few grew anxious, suspecting this to be the harbinger of some great calamity. Akmal Pradhan continued his efforts in the middle of all this. Using inspirational speeches, he tried to encourage people to come out of their homes. The villagers obeyed him, not because of his oratory, but out of the simple fear that if they didn't, it would anger the army. Within the hour, a group of about twenty men headed by Akmal Pradhan moved towards the camp. Kobej was among them. He had had no desire to be part of this group. He had tried to get out of it by asking why he must go as well, why did he need to see the military? Akmal Pradhan had scolded him into going.

Akmal Pradhan wielded a bamboo pole, which sported an overlarge Pakistani flag. Pradhan was having difficulty managing it because of the size. But he kept at it. He and his group moved forward chanting "Pakistan *zindabad*! Long live Pakistan!" But before they reached the camp, another procession showed up. The other procession was a little larger—about twenty-five men in all. They were led by Ramjan Sheikh, who was also holding a flag aloft. They were also chanting the "Pakistan *zindabad*!" slogan in chorus.

Akmal Pradhan was flabbergasted. He stood stock still, and because he stopped, so did his followers. But only for a moment. Gathering himself within seconds, he yelled even louder, "Pakistan *zindabad!*" This roused the spirit of his people, and even if their procession was the smaller of the two, they sounded louder. Both processions reached the camp at the same time.

The officer in charge of the Pakistani soldiers was young. A desk and chair had been brought from the school building and set up in front of a tent. The officer was sitting there. Both processions stopped at a distance from him. Neither Akmal Pradhan nor Ramjan Sheikh had the courage to come any closer. They stood immobile and tried to outdo each other in chanting slogans.

This went on for a while. When the officer finally stood up, both groups seemed to lose their rhythm. If one man began a chant, the others didn't take up the call. Or they responded out of beat, abruptly. The voices of a few sounded too loud; the voices of others, out of tune. The slight smile that played on the face of the Pakistani officer seemed to hint at his enjoyment of the scene.

The officer planted his hands on his hips and moved towards them. His smile had disappeared. When they saw the grim officer approach, both groups became flustered. Akmal Pradhan and Ramjan Sheikh yelled "Pakistan *zindabad!*" almost at the same time. At first, nobody responded to the call. Then, within a few seconds, all of them began shouting "Pakistan *zindabad!* Pakistan *zindabad!*" so discordantly that the officer raised his arms in surrender. The faint smile had returned to his lips. This made the villagers heave a collective sigh of relief. The officer reached them but did not stop. He circled them, sizing them up.

Neither of the groups paused for a moment in their sloganeering. The officer seemed annoyed; he gestured to a solider standing nearby. The soldier pointed his rifle at the sky and fired a single shot. As soon as the echo of the bullet died down, the entire area grew as silent as a grave. The men in the two groups felt as if their feet had suddenly sunk a foot into the ground. But this did not seem to inconvenience them. They seemed to enjoy standing motionless, rooted to the earth.

Their misery brought the faint smile back to the officer's lips. Once again, he began circling them, observing. Then he stopped abruptly. One by one, he looked into their faces. Akmal Pradhan and Ramjan Sheikh were clutching their Pakistani flags. The officer focussed his gaze on them. He stared at Ramjan Sheikh for a while. Then he looked at Akmal Pradhan. Akmal Pradhan stiffened under his gaze. He felt as if he couldn't take a single step. He desperately tried to keep himself under control. He cocked his head a little to the side and whispered to Kobej, who was standing next to him, "Kobej, why is he looking at me like that?"

"I don't know. How am I supposed to know?" Kobej spoke quite loudly. He did not like any of this. Just as he hadn't had the slightest desire to come here, he didn't want to remain here either.

In his head, he was furious with Akmal Pradhan. And now he was getting angry with the officer. *Shala*, what a show-off! Acting like a boss.

The officer returned to his chair. He pulled a pack of cigarettes out of his shirt pocket and lit up. Then he gestured with his finger for Akmal Pradhan and Ramjan Sheikh to approach him. At first, they were befuddled by his gesture. Their feet seemed to be rooted to the ground still. Then suddenly, they grew frantic, wriggling to free themselves of their invisible bonds and racing up to the officer. Their momentum prevented them from coming to a stop right away. Finally, they gathered themselves and offered salams that were practically salutes, saying, "*Assalamu 'alaykum,* sir."

The officer didn't respond to their greeting. His smile had disappeared. But his voice was gentle. "You are late, boys, you are late." Akmal Pradhan and Ramjan Sheikh smiled like idiots.

The officer said in broken Bengali, "It's been a while since I arrived here with my troop. But you're late. In fact, even after you came, you took too long to come and greet me. I don't think I like that."

Akmal Pradhan and Ramjan Sheikh's smiles disappeared.

"Are you surprised to hear me speak in Bengali?"

Akmal Pradhan and Ramjan Sheikh nodded. They were indeed quite surprised.

"Nothing to be surprised about. I've been in this region for a while now."

Pradhan and Sheikh smiled again.

"Learning new languages is my hobby. Bengali is actually quite a gentle language."

Pradhan and Sheikh laughed.

"Of course, Urdu is more melodious compared to Bengali."

Pradhan and Sheikh nodded vigorously in agreement.

"As I mentioned, languages are my hobby. I've noticed that as a Hindu language, Bengali is actually quite limited."

Pradhan and Sheikh continued to nod without comprehending any of this.

"But then there's no point in telling you any of this. You won't understand."

With smiles on their faces, Pradhan and Sheikh agreed to this as well—yes, they didn't understand.

"But I understand you." The officer continued. "I understand you Bengalis. You have no identity. You're a helpless and hopeless bunch. Now we're going to see if we can grant you an identity. That's why we're here."

Pradhan and Sheikh didn't understand. But a residue of their smiles remained on their faces.

The officer glanced at Ramjan Sheikh and Akmal Pradhan indifferently. A small smile pierced his indifference momentarily. In English, he said, "I can see you've divided into two groups. Very good. I can probably get a lot of information if I pit you against each other. I know you well, Bengali dogs, you're always at each other's throats all the time anyway. All I have to do is provoke you a little. You'll do the rest yourselves."

"What's your name?" The officer asked Akmal Pradhan. Akmal Pradhan couldn't believe it at first. The officer wanted to know his name? He glanced sideways at Ramjan Sheikh and said his name aloud.

"Are you Muslim?"

Akmal Pradhan felt hurt. Of course he was Muslim, one hundred percent, one million percent if needs be. Could sir not see his beard or the scar on his forehead from his constant namaz?

The officer evinced no interest in either the beard or the scar. Almost to himself, he said, "Tagore had a beard as well, it's easy enough to grow. A beard can just grow on its own, and that scar on the forehead—that could be a tumor or something. Anyway, who cares!" The officer asked, "Do you fast?"

Of course he fasted, affirmed Akmal Pradhan.

"When do you fast?"

He fasted during the month of Ramzan, Pradhan confirmed. He also fasted on special occasions.

The officer slapped him on the back. "Good. Verrrrry good."

Akmal Pradhan's smile almost split his face. Not sideways, this time he looked at Ramjan Sheikh square in the eyes. He looked back at his followers.

"Tell your men to sit down."

Pradhan turned around at once and gestured to his group to sit down. Everyone sat down on the ground except Kobej. Pradhan stared at him in mute helplessness. But Kobej paid no attention.

"Why can't you sit, Kobej?" Akmal Pradhan pleaded.

"I don't feel like it," Kobej said. But after a moment's hesitation, he sat.

"*Shala* is cracked," Pradhan muttered. "He'll be the end of me."

The officer had noted the entire exchange. He laughed a little. "Akmal, it looks like this fellow of yours isn't obedient enough. Perhaps a little arrogant."

Pradhan chortled like a fool.

"Still, I like men who are slightly arrogant. You don't find that among Bengalis."

The officer lit another cigarette. A loud hubbub arose nearby. They spotted a loud group of young boys approaching. The assistant headmaster of the school was leading them. When they came closer, it became clear that they were not merely shouting, they were singing. The song they were singing was the national anthem of Pakistan. The whole group came near and then began a fairly disordered march-past. The assistant headmaster saluted Akmal Pradhan first, and then the officer. The officer stared at him with distinct curiosity. "Who are you? What's your name?" Before the assistant headmaster could speak, Akmal Pradhan informed the officer that this was the assistant headmaster of the primary school and his name was Emdad Miah.

"And what is he doing?" the officer asked. Akmal Pradhan was taken aback. Could the officer not see what the assistant headmaster was doing? But before he could respond, a sliver of a smile appeared on the officer's face. "The national anthem, isn't it?"

Akmal Pradhan laughed in relief and nodded. Yes, it was indeed the national anthem. He also remembered to let the officer know that he was the one who had organised this anthem-singing. He mentioned that it was in accordance with his directions that the schoolboys sang the national anthem every morning before school.

"Really!" The officer's eyes danced with merriment. He turned to an underling and called him over, asking him something in a low voice.

The schoolboys were still giving the national anthem all they were worth. Some of them were marching, some weren't. Just as their feet were out of step, their voices were out of sync. The underling whom the officer had called stared at the boys for a few moments. After a couple of minutes, he said something to the officer, making him smile. "A bunch of clowns." He roared, "Silence!" The boys didn't quite understand, but they grew quiet when they heard him shout. As soon as they grew silent, they seemed to droop. A few wanted to sit down. The assistant head-master's glare put a stop to that.

"Who taught them the national anthem?" the officer asked.

Akmal Pradhan's face lit up with a smile. He mentioned again that he had organised it. Then he called Emdad Miah close. He pointed at him and said, "Him. He's the one responsible for teaching the boys to sing."

"You taught these boys how to sing the national anthem?" the officer asked in an easy voice.

Emdad Miah felt relieved. He nodded.

The officer took three steps to the right, then he turned and took three steps to the left. He walked to Ramjan Sheikh. "And what's your name?"

All the breath that Ramjan Sheikh had been holding in so far was expelled now. He told the officer his name. "Tell me something," the officer said in his easy tone. "Tell me the truth. Those boys—were they singing the national anthem correctly?"

Ramjan Sheikh didn't understand.

"Well, why are you silent? You tell me, were they singing correctly or did they make some mistakes?"

Ramjan Sheikh glanced at Akmal Pradhan. He said that the boys had not been singing correctly, they had made mistakes.

"They've made some mistakes with the words, sometimes even entire lines, right?"

Ramjan Sheikh agreed without understanding too much. Yes, mistakes.

"Therefore, the person who taught them the national anthem should be punished, right? Shouldn't he? What do you think?" The officer wasn't really curious about Ramjan Sheikh's thoughts on the matter. "Thank you, Ramjan Sheikh, for agreeing with me."

As soon as he was done talking, the officer looked at two of his soldiers. Then he looked at Emdad Miah. The soldiers fell upon him like wolves. They grabbed him from either side and suspended him in the air. They moved a little to the right. They threw Emdad Miah onto the ground, pulled out their weapons and shot him dead.

The whole thing happened with such speed and suddenness that at first no one really understood that a man had just been killed. Then the response was swift. Some of the students fainted; some screamed and wept in fear; some fled.

The grownups appeared perplexed about how to respond. They stood unmoving for a few moments, looking at one another in shock. Some of them crumpled, trembling, to the ground. None of this affected the army officer. He pointed at Akmal Pradhan and gestured at him to move closer. Akmal Pradhan didn't move. He had no desire to get any closer to the officer. Also, he felt as if his feet were bound to the earth. When the officer shouted suddenly, the bond was loosened. But he couldn't seem to come out of the witless state he was in. His body didn't want to respond. He glanced back at Kobej for a moment. Then, almost as though he didn't know what he was doing, he walked up to the officer. "You!" The officer's voice dripped with scorn. "You're the one who organised this national anthem? It's under your directions that these boys sang this song incorrectly, right?"

Akmal Pradhan howled and sobbed so hard it was unclear what he was trying to say.

"Enough. You don't have to say anything." The officer silenced Akmal Pradhan with a raised finger. "You're the one who taught the students the national anthem wrong. You should be punished, shouldn't you? What do you think?"

Akmal Pradhan broke down into desperate tears.

"All Bengalis are the same." The officer wrinkled his nose. "All they know is how to cry."

Akmal Pradhan's weeping intensified. "Shut up." The officer scolded mildly. "I'm forgiving you this time. But I have my doubts about whether you're a *sachcha* Pakistani." Akmal Pradhan wept even louder. He claimed he was a Pakistani, a true Pakistani. He was a Muslim, a true Muslim. The officer could ask for proof. He knew how to say his namaz, he fasted, he was going on the hajj pilgrimage next year, and he knew the kalimas. Did sir want to hear?

The officer wiggled his eyebrows. "Really! You know the kalimas?"

Yes, yes, he did, he knew them all. Should he recite them, all of them?

The officer hid his smile and nodded. "Begin."

Akmal Pradhan drew his breath. Then he began chanting the kalimas. At the end of each one, he looked at the officer's face. When he had completed all four, he stood there solemnly. The officer turned to Ramjan Sheikh. "What do you think? Do you think he recited the kalimas correctly?"

Ramjan Sheikh hesitated and looked at Akmal Pradhan. Then he nodded—Akmal Pradhan had indeed repeated the kalimas correctly.

"You know for sure?"

Ramjan Sheikh nodded, again, after a moment's hesitation.

"All right. Why don't *you* say them now?"

Ramjan Sheikh also drew in a deep breath. Then he too recited the kalimas one after another.

The officer turned to Akmal Pradhan. "Did you hear him?"

Akmal Pradhan nodded.

"Did he say them correctly?"

Akmal Pradhan also hesitated. He too glanced at Ramjan Sheikh. Then he too acknowledged helplessly that Ramjan Sheikh had recited them correctly too.

The officer chuckled and shrugged. "Good, that's good. Maybe you *are* Muslims." He laughed and asked Akmal Pradhan, "Do you know why I asked you whether Sheikh's kalimas were correct or not?" Akmal Pradhan shook his head fearfully.

The officer turned to Ramjan Sheikh and asked, "And do you know why I asked *you* whether Pradhan's kalimas were correct? Or do you not know either?"

Ramjan Sheikh shook his head. He didn't know either.

The officer started laughing again. "Because I don't know the kalimas."

Both Akmal Pradhan and Ramjan Sheikh stared at him in astonishment.

The officer lit another cigarette and said indifferently, "It makes no difference, really. Because I know how to shoot. I know how to kill those who are against us."

FOUR

That night, Akmal Pradhan shivered with fever. But he didn't want to pay any attention to it. He told Kobej in an uneasy voice, "Kobej, I told you so." Kobej wasn't happy. He hadn't said a single word since they had returned from the Pakistani army camp. The army officer had kindly allowed them to bring back Emdad Miah's corpse. The body had been buried that same evening. Kobej had dug the grave and had also participated in other rituals, such as bathing the dead body. He had not known he was capable of doing these things. But he hadn't said a single word the whole time. He had wanted to spend the rest of the day by himself. But Akmal Pradhan didn't allow it. Akmal Pradhan was not letting him out of sight for a single moment. Again and again he said the same thing, "Kobej, I told you so."

This repetition annoyed Kobej. Finally, he said, "You told me what?"

"Didn't I tell you?" Akmal Pradhan was surprised.

"First, you have to tell me what you told me."

Akmal Pradhan said he had told Kobej to finish off Ramjan Sheikh. But Kobej had paid no attention. Because he hadn't done it yet, yesterday Akmal Pradhan had been humiliated in front of all those people. All those people had witnessed the army officer scolding him. All those people had seen Akmal Pradhan cry like a baby.

"Why did you cry?" Kobej seemed even more annoyed.

Oh, he wasn't supposed to cry? Akmal Pradhan was incensed. Emdad Miah was shot dead without rhyme or reason, then he was told to approach the officer, and he wasn't supposed to cry? What would anyone else have done? Kobej did not answer Akmal Pradhan. He expressed surprise and sorrow at Emdad Miah's death. For the first time since it happened, Kobej opened his mouth on the subject. He looked at Akmal Pradhan with incomprehension in his eyes and said he still couldn't quite believe that Emdad Miah was dead, still couldn't figure out the reason why he had been killed.

Seeing Kobej so concerned about a single death irked Akmal Pradhan. He looked at Kobej with a serious expression and observed that Emdad Miah was dead because of Kobej.

"What did I do?" Kobej was astonished.

Akmal Pradhan immediately began to list all the things Kobej hadn't done. The upshot was that if Kobej had listened to him and got rid of Ramjan Sheikh, then Emdad Miah wouldn't have had to die and Akmal Pradhan wouldn't have had to suffer this humiliation.

Kobej knew Akmal Pradhan was right to some extent. So the boys had made some mistakes while singing. Was it possible to always sing a song perfectly? Was everyone capable of singing a song without making mistakes, like a radio artist did? But to kill someone, just because of mistakes in a song! All of Kobej's fury turned towards Ramjan Sheikh. Ramjan Sheikh was the one who had told the officer that there were mistakes in the song. He could have kept his mouth shut. Nothing would have happened to Ramjan Sheikh if he had stayed silent, but Emdad Miah would have survived.

Kobej's rage kept growing. Gradually, he felt the desire to tear Ramjan Sheikh apart, limb from limb. Akmal Pradhan somehow guessed his desire. He said that Ramjan Sheikh would now go on a rampage—he could even try to frame Kobej in some way.

Kobej didn't seem particularly perturbed by that prospect. He sat quietly biting his nails.

Akmal Pradhan was a little surprised. He was annoyed, but he asked in a gentle voice whether Kobej had given any thought to the proposed one thousand taka and small piece of land.

Kobej didn't respond to his question. Instead, he expressed surprise that the army officer did not know the kalimas.

Akmal Pradhan said nothing.

"If he doesn't know them himself, why did that fellow ask you to recite them?"

Akmal Pradhan didn't answer his question.

"And then he said something in English."

"Can *you* recite the kalimas?"

Kobej was irritated. "Why would I want to?"

Akmal Pradhan laughed. "Why would you want to? What if they ask you to?"

"Why would they ask me to?" Kobej looked at Akmal Pradhan in surprise.

"You don't think they will? Whether you're a Hindu or a Muslim . . ."

Kobej was seriously annoyed. "Don't tell me all this." He told Akmal Pradhan he had no interest in who was Hindu, who was Muslim, who was Pakistani or whatever.

"What are you saying?" Akmal Pradhan exclaimed. "You have no interest in who is Hindu or Muslim? Then who are you?"

"The things you say!" replied Kobej in a tone of astonishment. "I'm Kobej, of course."

The next day, when Akmal Pradhan showed up at the Pakistani army camp with Kobej, Ramjan Sheikh was already there. The officer was settled into a chair nearby, turning the pages of an English newspaper. In a chair next to him, though at a distance, sat a man. Ramjan Sheikh stood even farther, flanked by his men.

Akmal Pradhan was astonished to see the man in the second chair. He knew the man very well. He was some sort of cousin of the Joy Bangla leader at the *ganj*, the leader whose tune Hares Master used to dance to. They had a large family compound in the *ganj*, which housed the entire extended family. But what was he doing here? Had the army captured him? But if that was the case, why would he be sitting in a chair like he was a bigwig?

He knew who the man was, but Akmal Pradhan had never spoken to him. Now the fellow looked at him, wagged his eyebrows, and asked, "Well, Pradhan, how are you?" His dancing eyebrows and the question enraged Akmal Pradhan. "*Shala*, asking me how I am!" he muttered to himself. "Why should I tell you how I am?"

Such words could not be levelled at the man without knowing what exactly he was doing here. So Pradhan smiled and nodded. The officer put the newspaper on the table. He turned slightly towards Pradhan and gave a brief smile. "Pradhan, are you a late riser? Do you know how early Ramjan Sheikh showed up? Haven't you heard, early to bed, early to rise? And look: Sheikh has brought me a copy of the newspaper. It's two days old, but at least he brought it for me. Do you know what we call this? We call this efficiency. We like efficient people." Unable to figure out what he should say or do, Akmal Pradhan smiled foolishly.

"Okay, so hand it over."

Hand what over? Akmal Pradhan's foolish smile grew wider.

"The list, the list!"

What list? Akmal Pradhan didn't understand. He glanced at Ramjan Sheikh out of the corner of his eye. Ramjan Sheikh had a serious look on his face. This reassured him, but he was still angry with Ramjan Sheikh. Why had Sheikh arrived before him? Why was he trying to go over Akmal Pradhan's head to strike up a friendship with the army? But he didn't have time to ponder such things. The army officer was staring at him. Akmal Pradhan asked humbly what list was required of him.

The officer was disappointed. "Pradhan, you don't seem clever at all. Didn't I show you an example yesterday afternoon?

Couldn't you surmise what sort of list I might want? Think about it—what sort of list would I ask for?"

Akmal Pradhan remained silent.

"Ramjan Sheikh is a fool as well, just like you. He too failed to bring a list when he came here."

The *ganj* leader's cousin opened his mouth at this juncture. "Sir, these are uneducated men . . . "

"Uneducated men are the most dangerous, did you know that?"

"That may be so, sir," said the *ganj* leader's cousin. "But I know these men. They're innocent."

"Are you saying they're innocent because you're Bengali yourself?"

The leader's cousin seemed stung by the officer's words. "I'm not Bengali, sir, I'm Pakistani."

"What other choice do you have?" The officer said softly.

"Did you say something, sir?"

"Who is to make the list, then? These two bearded asses?"

"Wouldn't it be better to form the committee first, sir?"

The officer considered this for a few moments. "What's the point of this committee? These committees are useless. But, fine. Go ahead and form your committee."

The leader's cousin, whose name was Ali Akkas, as Akmal Pradhan and Ramjan Sheikh now found out, became very busy. He delivered a brief speech to Akmal Pradhan and Ramjan Sheikh explaining the current situation. He told them that the integrity of Pakistan had to be protected, no matter what the cost.

The kafirs who were working to destroy this golden Pakistan had to be stopped. Every person in every household must step forward to achieve this. (When he heard the bit about "every person in every household," Akmal Pradhan was tempted to ask, what news of your Joy Bangla leader cousin? But he couldn't quite muster the courage.) Ali Akkas said, "Praise be to Allah that the glorious Pakistani army has intervened at exactly the right juncture." However, the Pakistani army was not enough to deal with the evil activities of these kafirs and infidels. Hence, every region should create an organisation to assist the army. Peace and discipline in each area had to be maintained. And information about any anti-state activities had to be delivered to the rightful authorities, that is—the Pakistani army.

"For this, a committee must be formed. A Peace Committee." Akkas Ali paused to gather his breath after speaking for so long. After resting his voice a few moments, he resumed, "For now, the central office for the committee will be located in the *ganj*. This village, as well as five or six other neighbouring villages, will be under its jurisdiction. Pradhan, Ramjan, do you have any objections to joining this committee?"

Both of them agreed at once to join this committee. Both of them confirmed that there could be no possible reason *not* to join it. Because both of them would lay down their lives for Pakistan. So a fifteen-member committee dedicated to safeguarding the indivisibility of Pakistan and peace in the area was formed on the spot. Akmal Pradhan was nominated president and Ramjan Sheikh, general secretary, from their village. They then decided on thirteen others. Pradhan ardently wanted to include Kobej, but Ramjan Sheikh's baleful eyes forced him to abandon the idea.

Other than a couple of minor comments, the army officer had not said much so far. Once the committee had been finalised, he stretched and said, "I hope you two donkeys have realised by now what kind of list I'm expecting from you?"

No, neither Akmal Pradhan nor Ramjan Sheikh had worked it out yet. They kept quiet. Ali Akkas, the cousin of the *ganj*'s Joy Bangla leader, president of the regional Peace Committee, said, "Sir, may I explain it to them?"

The officer stopped him with a raised hand. "Uh-uh. You don't have to do anything. I'm enjoying talking to them . . . at least, as long as I don't lose my temper. You know I hate everything when I'm in a bad mood. No, actually, you don't. But I'm sure you'll find out. Anyway, Pradhan, Sheikh, tell me, what do you think you'll have to do as president and general secretary of the Peace Committee?"

What was it that Ali Akkas had told them? It was just a few minutes ago. They had no difficulty remembering. With smiling faces, they declared that their job was to ensure the integrity of Pakistan and peace in their localities.

"If peace is—or may be—compromised, or something has happened—or may happen—that could result in the loss of peace, you're supposed to report that to the army as well, right?"

Of course. Both of them nodded vigorously.

"So, now, tell me. What list should you be giving me?"

Akmal Pradhan still didn't get it. Ramjan Sheikh did, but he hesitated. He didn't say anything to the officer, but turned towards Ali Akkas. He asked Ali Akkas, "Is sir asking for a list of people who are infidels, kafirs, those who do not want an undivided Pakistan, those who are Joy Bangla?"

Ali Akkas nodded joyfully. The officer said, "Good, Sheikh, good.

You're not as big a fool as I thought you were. But, Pradhan, you . . . " the officer turned towards him, "you are truly a fool. We should not have made you the president of the Peace Committee. Should we withdraw the appointment? No, let's give you another chance."

Ali Akkas and Ramjan Sheikh busied themselves right away. Akmal Pradhan turned to look at Kobej, who stood right behind him. "*Shala* pulled a fast one on me."

"But you're the one who couldn't answer properly," said Kobej.

"Kobej, you're taking Sheikh's side as well?" Pradhan seemed hurt.

"Don't say that! I'm not on Sheikh's side."

"You didn't do what I told you to. Now look at what's happened."

Before Kobej could respond, Ali Akkas called Akmal Pradhan over. Pradhan whispered a prayer under his breath and went to him. The three of them put together a list. The very first name on that list was Hares Master's. The handful of people who had left with Hares Master were also on that list. These names were easy. It took Akmal Pradhan and Ramjan Sheikh longer to add other names, because this required a little more thought.

They tried to remember which of the villagers had opposed them or disobeyed them at different times. They also took note of names of people who might become dangerous in the future. However, a few names got crossed out because when Akmal Pradhan wanted them on the list, Ramjan Sheikh didn't, or vice versa. Gradually, a fairly long list came together. Ali Akkas carried it over to where the officer sat with his feet on the table.

Akmal Pradhan moved away from Ramjan Sheikh to stand beside Kobej, who asked, "Did you make the list?"

"I did. I couldn't get Idris's name in there. But I got Hares's."

While they had been busy making the list, Kobej had found out that Ali Akkas was related to the *ganj* Joy Bangla leader and they lived in the same house. "So, when you made this list, did you include the *ganj* leader's name?"

"He doesn't belong to our area," Akmal Pradhan told him solemnly.

Kobej chuckled. He told Akmal Pradhan to ask Ali Akkas if the *ganj* leader's name was on the list that had been compiled.

He couldn't do it too loudly, so Akmal Pradhan scolded Kobej in a low voice. "Kobej, you paid no attention to what I said . . . "

Kobej chuckled again. "Why are you changing the subject?"

Their brief chat ended there because the officer had lowered his feet

from the table and stood up.

A small group of Pakistani soldiers set out. Pradhan and Sheikh were in charge of taking them around and pointing out houses and routes. A handful of other men trailed behind them, some willingly, some not. Pradhan had made sure that Kobej came along. Kobej had actually had no desire to go with this group. But Pradhan was keeping a careful eye on him.

As they walked ahead, the young officer said to Ali Akkas, "I'm losing my temper. I've warned you about what happens when I lose my temper."

Ali Akkas gulped and said, "This is a very peaceful village, sir. There's never been an untoward incident here. I live practically next door; I know."

"Really? If that's the case, why are there so many names on this list that Pradhan and Sheikh have drawn up?"

Ali Akkas was quiet.

The officer called to Pradhan and Sheikh. "Listen, you two. You know what Akkas is saying? He's saying this is a very peaceful village. Nothing untoward happens here. Is he right?"

Akmal Pradhan couldn't figure what his response should be. But Ramjan Sheikh answered right away. He said there wasn't a single village in East Pakistan where a couple of bad incidents hadn't taken place, because those infidels were trying to stir up trouble everywhere. One or two minor bad things had happened in their village as well. But he—Ramjan Sheikh—had tried to stop such things. And now that 'officer sir' had arrived, they had nothing to worry about at all.

"Good," said the officer. "I have no idea whether you actually believe what you're saying or whether you're just saying it for my benefit. But whichever it is, you will go far, Ramjan Sheikh, because you are very clever."

Ramjan Sheikh laughed unabashedly at this. Behind them, Akmal Pradhan glared at Kobej. Kobej looked away. He was dying to light a bidi. But Akmal Pradhan had cautioned him strongly not to smoke in front of the officer. Now he just wanted to abandon this group so that he could go somewhere and smoke his bidi. He didn't understand any of this Peace Committee business anyway. What did he care about what had happened in far off places? He had no desire to run alongside everyone else and the army, trying to save Pakistan. He felt angry at Akmal Pradhan. But he also felt a little sorry for him. The man was constantly losing out to Ramjan Sheikh.

The small group of army men soon reached Hares Master's home. Ramjan Sheikh showed them the way. If Ramjan Sheikh hadn't led them, it would have been Akmal Pradhan, or someone else, perhaps. But now the officer was happy with Ramjan Sheikh. So he was assigning all these jobs to him. Ramjan Sheikh was over the moon. Leading the soldiers, he looked closely at all the houses. Most of them had their doors and windows shuttered, as word had travelled that the military was out. But this didn't disappoint Ramjan Sheikh because he knew that, whether through the slats of a fence, or an opening in the door, or a slightly ajar window, everyone was watching the army follow Ramjan Sheikh.

There was no one in the house other than Hares Master's widowed mother and his little sister, who was barely thirteen. The officer seemed surprised. "These two are Hares Master's only family? There's no one else?"

Ramjan Sheikh shook his head vehemently. There was no one else. He was sure.

"That Master, he's gone off with those infidels, leaving these two behind?"

"Yes, sir, that's what he's done."

"No responsibility towards his family! He should be punished."

"Yes sir, if we could catch him, we'd punish him ourselves."

"But for now, we must punish his mother for giving birth to such an infidel. Right?"

Ali Akkas was silent, Akmal Pradhan was silent; it was only Ramjan Sheikh who agreed enthusiastically with the officer.

A soldier shot Hares Master's widowed mother dead. Their house was set on fire. Hares's thirteen-year-old sister was to face no punishment for now. She would be dealt with later, when the officer so desired. For now, she was placed in Ramjan Sheikh's custody. Ramjan Sheikh sent Idris to take the girl to his house.

The small group of soldiers worked quickly. One by one, they visited the houses of those whose names were on the list. They picked up those who were home; if they couldn't find them, they took a brother or a father. The homes of the three young men who had left with Hares Master were set on fire. If anyone attempted to flee the blazing houses, they were promptly shot down. A few were allowed to run a little distance first. Sort of like target practice.

Many villagers watched. Those who didn't see it heard the steady sound of shooting. Wails rose in every single household in the village. No one tried to escape. There *was* no escape. The military had set up a tent in the direction of the escape route. Seven soldiers were stationed there day and night.

When the shooting stopped, the noise of weeping reached the officer's ears. In a sombre voice he asked, "Why are people crying? Are they mourning these dead kafirs?"

After a long silence, Akmal Pradhan spoke up. "No, no. They have no grief for those kafirs. No, they're crying out of fear."

The officer scolded him "You stay quiet. You know nothing. Ramjan, you speak."

Ramjan Sheikh hesitated and said, "Actually, sir, it's probable that they are crying out of fear."

The officer creased his forehead. "Why would they cry in fear?

What do they have to fear? We're here to keep them safe. If they're not supporting the infidels, they should have nothing to fear."

Ali Akkas, Akmal Pradhan and Ramjan Sheikh—all three of them kept quiet.

The officer was annoyed. "Tell them to stop. I can't stand the noise of weeping. It makes me lose my temper."

So Ramjan Sheikh and Akmal Pradhan sent a few of their men to every house. They were to tell people that Pakistanis had nothing to fear. The only ones being punished were those who had not remained loyal to Pakistan, those who had become infidels, traitors. Kobej insisted that he go with this team. Akmal Pradhan glared at him, but couldn't stop him.

When they didn't find many of the people who were on the list, the officer grew angry. He kept shouting at Ali Akkas, Akmal Pradhan and Ramjan Sheikh. They kept repeating that only a handful had escaped and it didn't matter since they would never be able to come back to the village again.

"They can go to other villages and create bases there, isn't that the case?" The officer shouted.

"No, no, there aren't all that many villages nearby," they tried to reassure the officer. The officer turned to them and suddenly exploded. "You bastards! You think I don't understand anything? You think I don't know where these infidels are launching attacks? You *know*, you know everything—where they are, where their camps are."

For a long while, none of them spoke, not even Akkas. Gradually, Akkas gathered his courage. He swore in the name of Allah, in the name of Pakistan, that none of them had that information. If they did, they would certainly have divulged it. But they would inform the officer as soon as they found out. Of this, the officer could be sure.

The officer's anger did not abate. But, in a surprisingly calm voice, he told them that he had received news that the infidels had launched an attack along the length of the border about three villages away. They had information that such criminal actions were increasingly moving from the border areas to the inner regions. They had information. They knew everything. What they didn't know with certainty were the identities of the people committing these acts. He pointed at Ali Akkas, Akmal Pradhan and Ramjan Sheikh. "So, that's the information you need to gather. Find out what locations the infidels are using to plan their moves." The three of them nodded. They knew quite clearly that this was their responsibility. The officer had no reason to be anxious.

In the meantime, the small team of soldiers, their killing done, had completed the looting phase of their operation. However, other than a few cows and goats, there wasn't too much plunder. They hadn't found anything they wanted. Gathering their meagre pickings together, they headed for camp. Ali Akkas,

Akmal Pradhan and Ramjan Sheikh followed them. Before they had gone too far, however, the officer asked them to turn back. He said he was feeling unhappy and didn't even want to see their faces right then.

So they stopped and turned back. At the last moment, Ramjan Sheikh steeled himself and blurted out his proposal. The officer thought it over for a few seconds. Then, with a small nod of the head, he agreed. Yes, tonight he would dine at Ramjan Sheikh's house.

FIVE

Akmal Pradhan couldn't locate Kobej when he returned home. This put him in a foul mood. He yelled at everyone in the house for no reason, making them nervous. His youngest wife, his favourite, got such a scolding when she came to him that she left in hiccups, trying to control her tears. At another time Akmal Pradhan would have busied himself consoling her. But right now he didn't even look at her twice. He didn't sit down to eat, even after many requests. Unsettled, he paced the small passageway in front of his bedchamber.

Kobej returned about an hour later. When he spotted Kobej, Akmal Pradhan began stuttering in rage. "Where . . . where were you?"

Kobej didn't answer.

"Why don't you speak? Where did you go?" Akmal Pradhan was practically jumping up and down in anger. The next instant, he demanded to know why Kobej hadn't returned home as soon as he was done with going house to house, reassuring people that loyal Pakistanis would come to no harm.

Kobej said that he hadn't felt like coming back.

"Didn't feel like it—you think that was reason enough?" Akmal Pradhan asked. Did Kobej know what disaster had befallen them?

Kobej shook his head. He didn't. And furthermore, he didn't care.

"Why don't you want to know?" Akmal Pradhan's anger remained unabated. Kobej was ignorant of the fact that Ramjan Sheikh had invited the officer to dinner that night and that the officer had accepted, pleased. If Kobej only knew, he would understand the disaster that was about to strike. The two of them together could now . . .

Kobej said, "Those two sons-of-pigs make quite a pair."

Akmal Pradhan was taken aback for a moment. Then a small smile blossomed on his lips. Why didn't Kobej finish off one of those sons-of-pigs?

Kobej turned to look Akmal Pradhan in the eye. Then, as if he were changing the subject, he asked why the military had killed Hares Master's widowed mother.

Akmal Pradhan raised a finger to his lips. "Shut up, Kobej. You won't understand."

Kobej laughed and said that was precisely why he was asking.

Akmal Pradhan hesitated. He seemed a little annoyed. Then, as if he were talking to a child, he said, "Why shouldn't the military kill Hares Master's mother! Why couldn't she control her son? A mother whose son became an infidel, joined forces with those who want to rip this nation apart—a mother like that should undoubtedly die."

Kobej laughed as though this was very funny. Still smiling, he asked, "The others who were killed—what had they done?"

Akmal Pradhan was irked. "Why are you asking all these questions, Kobej?"

Kobej laughed again. He said he wanted to try and look at things the way Akmal Pradhan and Ramjan Sheikh did.

Akmal Pradhan waved his hand at him to shut him up. "What have you decided, Kobej?"

"What are you referring to?"

"Don't you want the money? Aren't you going to take the land?"

Kobej replied grimly that Ramjan Sheikh had egged the army on to shoot Hares Master's mother.

Akmal Pradhan sighed in disappointment. Wearily, he said, "Today, the officer called Ramjan Sheikh clever, told him he would go far. Me, he shouted at." Why didn't Kobej understand that if things continued like this, there would soon be no Akmal Pradhan. And if there were no Akmal Pradhan, there would be no Kobej either.

Kobej remained silent for a few seconds and then smiled. "I'm thinking."

"Thinking! Thinking!" Akmal Pradhan was furious. "Still singing that song. Your thoughts will slide right out of your arse, you son of a bitch."

"They won't." Kobej lit a bidi. "They won't slide out of my arse. I'll keep my ass tight."

Ramjan Sheikh had made grand arrangements. Even Akmal Pradhan was impressed. He knew that Sheikh had done quite well the last few years and had bought up several small parcels of land. But he hadn't realised how well off Ramjan Sheikh was. It didn't make him angry though, it made him jealous. And furious with Kobej.

Ramjan Sheikh smiled broadly when he spotted Akmal Pradhan. He led him ceremoniously to a seat. He even spoke to Kobej with a smile. He left Pradhan and Kobej seated next to each other and busied himself elsewhere. He had much to do. Not everyone in the village had been invited; there had been no reason to invite them all. But that didn't mean Sheikh wasn't busy. An army officer would set foot in his house tonight—the very first visit to a house in their village—so he had to make sure nothing was amiss.

It was quite a large, open space, surrounded on all sides by Ramjan Sheikh's house. Right now, it was covered with an awning. An old-fashioned chair, much like a throne, had been set out on the northern side. In front of it was a table decorated with a pair of vases. Akmal Pradhan had seen a similar set-up at an award ceremony in the *ganj*. Clearly, Ramjan Sheikh had attended the same event.

Pradhan sat for a while with his eyes shut. He didn't feel like looking at any of it. But how could he not? How long could he stay there with his eyes closed? He opened his eyes, rose from his chair, looked at Kobej and sighed. Then he slowly walked towards Ramjan Sheikh. He had considered the issue and decided now was not the time to remain disengaged. Even if this was Ramjan Sheikh's house, he should help Sheikh with some of the work. Sheikh should know that he too was keeping his eye open to ensure the officer's comfort. The officer arrived with his team about an hour later. Ramjan Sheikh himself had gone to fetch them. Akmal Pradhan had hoped to go too, but Sheikh had avoided him. Since then, Pradhan had been feeling a little dispirited. So even when the officer arrived, he couldn't bring himself to put on a bright smile.

The officer slapped him on the back. "What's this, Pradhan, why so solemn? Don't you know that when fools act serious, they look like even bigger fools?" This deflated Akmal Pradhan further. The officer slapped his back again. "Cheer up, my boy! You can assume I rather like fools!"

Akmal Pradhan smiled but felt no better.

The food wasn't served right away. First, there were speeches. Since the officer was a guest in his house, Ramjan Sheikh wanted him to address everyone, to make a speech. He couldn't ask the officer directly, so Ramjan Sheikh himself started it off. He began his speech by berating the infidels and the leaders who had become kafirs. He said, "They will burn in the eternal fires of hell." It was true that there was a provision for all sinners to gain access to heaven, after experiencing hellfire. But he was pretty certain that Allah wouldn't forgive those who wanted to break up Pakistan, so they would be stuck in hell and never ascend to paradise.

He paused for breath, taking a moment to clear his throat. Then he began praising the Pakistani army. "The Pakistani troops have been sent at exactly the right moment. Like a gift from Allah. It is His unending beneficence—the military has come forward to save the nation. No infidel will be spared. Those who speak of Joy Bangla will be wiped out completely. This is what our faith dictates." Ramjan Sheikh paused again to catch his breath. He smiled and looked to his right, to the officer sitting a little behind him. "What can I say about this officer?" Ramjan Sheikh began again. Never in his life had he seen an army officer so smart and active, so devout; and he wouldn't see the likes of such an officer again. He offered up thanks to Allah for sending such an officer to their village.

Ramjan Sheikh kept talking. None of the Pakistani soldiers were paying attention. A few glanced at him now and then, but most of the time, they were busy joking and chatting amongst themselves. The officer was doing pretty much the same. Ali Akkas sat beside him, though at a respectful distance. The officer's relationship with Ali Akkas didn't involve joking and laughing together, so most of the time he sat quietly, as if rapt in thought. The officer glanced at Ramjan Sheikh now and then with curious, amused eyes.

After Ramjan Sheikh, it was Ali Akkas's turn to speak. He was smart. He had noticed what had been going on during Ramjan Sheikh's speech. So he kept it very short. Akmal Pradhan was dying to speak too. He knew quite well that Ramjan Sheikh was not going to call on him. So he stood up with the intention of taking the initiative himself. But Ramjan Sheikh pretended not to see him and said quickly, "And now, our esteemed guest will make a speech."

The officer himself was surprised at this announcement. He pointed at his own chest and said, "Me, make a speech? You're asking me to address everyone?"

"Yes, sir, you," Ramjan Sheikh said with a smile.

"I don't make speeches, do you understand? It's the Bengalis who make speeches, every chance they get. *We* get things done." The officer spoke cuttingly.

Ramjan Sheikh was taken aback. What was this? He seemed to have offended the chief guest by asking him to make a speech. Unable to decide on a course of action, he stood there like a fool. It was Ali Akkas who salvaged the moment. He said to the officer, "Sir, it's not like that. Of course we know that you people get things done. But, sir, since you're here, you should say something about our situation."

So the officer had to stand up. He said he was hoping for full cooperation from everyone. He liked their village so far.

He was assuming that, other than a handful of Infidels, everyone else was a Pakistani. So they too must desire the capture of these infidels.

If the villagers aided him in saving Pakistan, he would consider them good people. If they didn't, he would have no choice but to turn this village into hell.

When the officer was done, Ramjan Sheikh and Ali Akkas stood up and began to applaud. Copying them, the other villagers also stood up. So did Akmal Pradhan and Kobej. They too clapped without pause. Except that Kobej took a moment to whisper, "That damned Ramjan Sheikh is making us dance like monkeys."

"You're saying this now? I told you so!" Akmal Pradhan whispered back. He continued: if Kobej still didn't consider his proposal and come to a decision, in a few days, Ramjan Sheikh would indeed be banging out a beat on a *doogdoogi* to which they would have to dance. Many people in the village would probably pay good money to see the two of them dance like monkeys.

The food was brought out. Akmal Pradhan was surprised at what a rich spread Ramjan Sheikh had rustled up at such short notice. Beef, mutton, chicken and kababs of all sorts—and, of course, polao was mandatory.

There were no tables or seating arrangements for the common soldiers. Yes, there was a long table in front of them, but it was piled with food. The soldiers could squeeze themselves in to sit at it with their plates if they wanted. The officer didn't have to do any of this. A place had been set up for him where he was already sitting and he could eat right there. The food he was served had a few extra delicacies. It included some roasted chicken and a roasted leg of goat.

Once the food had been served, Ramjan Sheikh stood humbly beside the officer, holding a wash basin and a water jug. The officer washed his hands. He looked this way and that and called Akmal Pradhan near. Pradhan didn't understand why he was being summoned. When he came close, the officer asked in a surprised voice, "Pradhan, why are you sitting so far away? Are you offended by me?"

Akmal Pradhan bit his tongue. The things sir said! How could an inconsequential person like him sit next to someone like sir!

"I see you're not really a fool." The officer chuckled. "Anyway, Ramjan Sheikh, hand him a clean plate . . . Yes, Pradhan, wash your hands. You will sit and eat with me tonight. Sheikh, you don't mind, do you?"

Ramjan Sheikh put his palms together and shook his head. "Of course not! Of course not! Everything will be exactly the way sir wants."

"I want you to sit with us too."

Ramjan Sheikh did not wait. Assigning supervisory responsibilities to Idris, he washed his hands and sat down next to Akmal Pradhan. Impassively, the officer pulled their plates closer and dished out helpings of each item. He pushed the plates towards them and instructed, "Eat." Akmal Pradhan and Ramjan Sheikh looked at each other.

"Eat, both of you." The officer sounded grim. "I want to watch you eat." They didn't dare delay any longer. Lowering their heads, they began eating. The officer watched. Seemingly satisfied after a few minutes, he pulled his own plate closer. He served himself and then looked around at his troop. Then he began eating. None of the soldiers had started on their food yet. Once the officer began to eat, so did they. But several of them sat unmoving. They would eat later.

After dinner, most of the troops returned to their field camp. Food was sent to the soldiers who had remained at the camp, as well as to the seven who were stationed at the temporary camp in the north. Ramjan Sheikh and Akmal Pradhan organised all this together. Ramjan Sheikh didn't really want Akmal Pradhan around him, but he couldn't say so directly.

Having escorted the troops back to the camp, Akmal Pradhan and Ramjan Sheikh returned. The officer was still at Sheikh's house; Akmal Pradhan wanted to remain there as long as the officer was there. When they returned from the camp, they found out that he had decided to spend the night at Sheikh's house. Apparently he didn't feel like leaving after all that food, and he hadn't slept in a soft bed in a long while.

Ramjan Sheikh was in seventh heaven when he heard this. He looked at Akmal Pradhan and smiled. Pradhan smiled back but immediately retreated to stand beside Kobej.

"You see, Kobej?" he said in a wan voice.

"I see," Kobej replied.

Akmal Pradhan heaved a long sigh. "Just watch," he said. Kobej could just keep on watching, sure, he didn't have to do anything, he should just watch. When Idris had moved ahead and Kobej was left behind, then, and only then, would he get it. He would realise what a mistake he had made in not listening to Akmal Pradhan . . .

Before Akmal Pradhan finished, the officer waved for him and Kobej to come closer. Kobej didn't want to go but Akmal Pradhan almost dragged him there by the hand.

"Listen," the officer said, "we have to make a decision. That sister of Hares Master's, the one we caught this morning—what should we do about her?"

What was there to be done about her? Let her stay at Ramjan Sheikh's house till Hares Master returned to the village. And if he never returned, they could collectively make some sort of arrangement for her. This was Kobej's opinion and he was about to say it.

But Ramjan Sheikh lowered his head and whispered in the officer's ear before Kobej could speak. The officer's face lit up.

82

"Really? Why didn't you say so before? Now that you mention it, I've had a brainwave."

Akmal Pradhan looked eagerly at the officer and Ramjan Sheikh.

He regretted backing away a few moments ago to go up to Kobej. He would have known what the officer and Ramjan Sheikh were planning. Ramjan Sheikh whispered some more to the officer. The officer stood up, nodded, and, lighting a cigarette, began pacing. He stopped when he had smoked half of it. "Is the boy from this village? Is he here now?"

Ramjan Sheikh nodded. Of course he was. The officer walked up to Ramjan Sheikh. "Then have him brought here. Let their wedding be arranged. Let there be a happy occasion."

Akmal Pradhan didn't understand. Whom did the officer want brought over? What happy occasion? Pradhan glanced at Kobej. "Any idea what's going on?" But Kobej had no desire to find out. He wanted to go home.

Akmal Pradhan figured it out soon, though. There had been talk in the village about the muezzin marrying Hares Master's sister. Apparently they had promised their hearts to each other. Not too many details were public knowledge, but the muezzin liked Hares Master's sister Hawa a *lot*. The wedding would probably have taken place already, but Hares Master had become preoccupied with Joy Bangla, which delayed things. Now the officer was apparently set to get Hawa married to the muezzin. Someone had been sent to get him. The wedding would take place when he arrived.

Akmal Pradhan didn't like the idea for two reasons. First, an event was about to take place at Ramjan Sheikh's house under the aegis of the officer. Pradhan knew with a certainty that Sheikh was going to claim all credit for this. And the villagers would praise him to the skies. Which meant that Ramjan Sheikh was again a step ahead of him. Second, why should an army officer involve himself in things like weddings? Was this a suitable occupation for the military? What nonsense! Akmal Pradhan was annoyed, but there was nothing he could do. He glanced at Kobej and stood back quietly. Idris had gone to bring the muezzin. He returned with him within minutes. Idris had told the muezzin nothing. He had no idea what he had done wrong, so he looked, uncomprehending, at each of them in turn. Ramjan Sheikh assuaged his fears. He told the muezzin to touch the officer's feet, since he would be getting married to Hawa Bibi soon, owing to the kindness of this officer.

None of this seemed to make any difference to the muezzin. He didn't move forward to touch the officer's feet. He kept looking around, just as he had earlier, like a fool. Akmal Pradhan went up to him. He took the muezzin by the hand and led him to the officer. He told the officer, "This young man is *imandaar*, a man of faith. A true Muslim." When the officer smiled, he pushed the muezzin downward. "Do the salam, touch his feet." Pradhan kept his hold on the muezzin. When the muezzin was back on his feet, Pradhan told him, "Why don't you tell the officer I was the one who told you to chant the azan, my boy?"

"When?"

"When we heard the military had reached the *ganj*."

The muezzin remembered and prepared to tell the officer. But, at that moment, the officer began speaking. He wanted to know who would perform the wedding. Akmal Pradhan could do it, and he said as much. But Ramjan Sheikh proclaimed his desire to officiate in an even louder voice. So he was assigned the responsibility. In the meantime, Hawa was being prepared inside the house. The young woman had not said a single word since that morning. She had fainted several times; the rest of the time, she stared vacantly at some part of the room. Even now, the news that she was about to get married evoked no response. When she was brought outside, where the wedding was to take place, she kept looking around her in distress.

A faint smile appeared on the officer's lips when he saw her. "She's pretty, isn't she?" It seemed he was asking himself. And so he answered himself. "Yup. She's pretty, no doubt." He turned to Ramjan Sheikh. "Ramjan Sheikh, do you understand, we're about to do a good deed."

Ramjan Sheikh smiled. "How can there be any doubt?"

"We are bringing a Hindu girl into the sacred fold of Islam."

"Hindu?" Ramjan Sheikh looked at him in surprise. Akmal Pradhan was also surprised, as was the soon-to-be-married muezzin and everyone else present. The officer seemed astonished at their surprise. He seemed annoyed as well. "Didn't that Hares Master of yours go and join Joy Bangla?"

He had indeed. This could not be denied. But what was the point in repeating it? If they ever got their hands on Hares Master, they'd be sure to teach him a suitable lesson.

When they remained quiet, the officer shouted, "Why are you silent? You bunch of clowns. Tell me, if Hares Master goes and joins Joy Bangla, doesn't that make him a Hindu?"

This was also true. Hindu, definitely. Hares Master was now indeed a Hindu.

"So what does that mean? Is Hares Master's sister a Hindu or a Muslim?"

"Hindu! Hindu!" Several of them said at the same time.

The officer laughed. "So we're converting a Hindu into a Muslim.

Thanks to Ramjan Sheikh. He's the one who gave me the idea."

Ramjan Sheikh could barely contain his smile. He said again and again, no, no, all the credit belonged to 'officer sir.' The wedding was only taking place because of the officer's efforts.

"All right, why don't you perform the wedding now? Let me watch how you turn a Hindu girl into a Muslim. Go ahead, Sheikh, begin."

A large wooden stool had been brought out and placed in the yard. Someone had spread a red cloth with a floral print over it. The muezzin and Hawa Bibi were seated on the stool side by side. Ramjan Sheikh sat down facing them. He formally asked who would act as witnesses to the wedding. Witnesses? To the wedding? The officer volunteered immediately and chose Akmal Pradhan to act as second witness.

Ramjan Sheikh began conducting the wedding. A pair of old paper garlands had been sent in from the inner quarters of his household. Ali Akkas stood to one side, holding the garlands. Once the ceremony was over, he was going to hand the garlands to Hawa Bibi and the muezzin. They were supposed to place the garlands around each other's necks.

Ramjan Sheikh didn't take very long. When he was done, he looked at the officer. He said, "Since sir himself is a witness, there is no need to document anything. Everyone has seen sir act as a witness. The *den-mohr* for this marriage has been determined at three hundred and one taka. The muezzin and Hawa Bibi are now legally husband and wife. They may commence their conjugality."

When he concluded, the officer stood up. He lit a cigarette and released a big puff of smoke. "It would've been better if this wedding had taken place in the Hindu style. All of you already know how Hindu weddings work. Or, I should say how *your* weddings work. Why didn't you do it that way?"

Nobody replied.

"You know what, after seeing all of you, I too suddenly want to become a Hindu."

Akkas, Pradhan and Sheikh stared at the officer, but because they weren't exactly sure what he was saying, they kept quiet.

"What else to do but convert, you know? When in Rome and all that."

Ramjan Sheikh asked with some trepidation whether he should arrange to send the newly married couple to the muezzin's house.

"Yes, of course, of course," the officer nodded. "Send the muezzin off. Of course you don't need to make any arrangements. He can go by himself. Yes, tell him he can leave now."

Should he ask or was it a bad idea? Ramjan Sheikh hesitated and then asked anyway. Hawa Bibi—shouldn't Hawa Bibi be sent off with the muezzin?

As if he were shaking himself out of his languor, the officer asked, "Where have you arranged for me to sleep?" Ramjan Sheikh pointed out the room. The officer said, "Send Hawa Bibi to my room. I'll go in a little later." A strange silence descended. Ali Akkas, Akmal Pradhan and Ramjan Sheikh exchanged glances. The muezzin stared at the officer in sheer astonishment.

"Are you surprised at what I said? Say something. Don't just stand there like clowns."

But no one said a word.

The officer shouted, "Did someone rip out your tongues? Is that why you can't talk? Or do none of you understand what I'm saying?" Finally, Ramjan Sheikh forced a smile on his face. He said there was no reason not to understand what the officer was saying. He would instruct the muezzin to leave right away and send Hawa Bibi to the officer's room. He turned to the muezzin. The officer stopped him. "First, listen to me. I'm a reasonable man. I do nothing without a reason. You might be wondering why I'm having the girl sent to my room. Look, a Hindu girl has become a Muslim because of me. This upgradation took place solely because of me. So, naturally, she owes me something. You can also think of me as a Hindu priest. I've heard that the Hindu religion has a custom where Hindu brides spend their wedding night with the priest. So isn't it natural that Hawa Bibi should spend her wedding night with me?"

Ali Akkas and Ramjan nodded while the officer was speaking. Natural, quite natural. There was nothing unusual about this at all. Akmal Pradhan smiled broadly and said sir didn't need to say anything. There was no need to explain any of this to them. Because when no explanation was given, they would simply assume that whatever sir did was right.

The officer looked at Akmal Pradhan with deep admiration. "No, I truly misjudged you, Pradhan. You are indeed intelligent. You've got it exactly right—everything I do is correct, don't you think?"

It wasn't just Akmal Pradhan. This time Ramjan Sheikh and Ali Akkas nodded as well.

The officer raised his voice slightly. "Then be quick about it."

Hawa Bibi was still not in her senses. She understood nothing of what was going on. At Ramjan Sheikh's gesture, someone grabbed her and led her forward. Hawa Bibi showed no resistance and walked with him. Everyone watched indifferently, as if this were an everyday sight, not even worth noting. But the scene, which was scrolling like an endless image, was suddenly ripped apart. The muezzin startled everyone by shouting, "Where are you taking her?"

Ramjan Sheikh went up to him quickly, grabbing his arm. He told him something in a low voice. But the muezzin paid no attention and shouted again, "Where are you taking Hawa?"

The officer's brow creased at the noise. "What is he saying?"

"Nothing, sir," Akkas, Ramjan and Akmal said together. "Nothing."

"Why are you taking Hawa into that room?" The muezzin tried to free his arm from Ramjan Sheikh's grasp and run to Hawa. Ramjan Sheikh grabbed him from the back. Seeing this, Kobej suddenly made as if to go to them.

"Where do you think you're going?" Akmal Pradhan blocked his way.

Kobej looked at Akmal Pradhan with unwavering eyes. "Why are you standing in my way?"

"Mad, you've gone mad, Kobej." Pradhan pulled him away. The officer noticed none of this. His attention was focused on Ramjan Sheikh and the muezzin. He watched for a while, as though he was vastly amused. In a gentle voice he asked, "Sheikh, doesn't he want to leave?"

"Of course he does, sir, why wouldn't he?" Ramjan Sheikh tried to reassure him.

"No, I won't go," the muezzin shouted. His voice seemed to push Ramjan Sheikh back.

Ali Akkas and a few other men rushed over. Before they reached him, however, a couple of soldiers grabbed the muezzin. But the muezzin wouldn't back down. He looked with loathing at the officer. "You *haramkhor* son of a bitch, let her go! Let my wife go!"

The officer seemed startled at first but gradually, a smile grew on his face. "He's a brave one—courageous. I've never seen this among submissive Bengalis." Still smiling, he pulled his gun out of its holster and pointed it at the muezzin. But then he laughed and holstered it again. "No, no, not now, not now. It can be done later on. And that will be funnier, I think." At his signal, the two soldiers pulled the muezzin out of sight.

The officer didn't wait any longer. Without sparing a glance at anyone, he entered the room where Hawa Bibi was and shut the door.

That night, Pradhan stayed over at Ramjan Sheikh's house. He was coming to the realisation that he was gradually being pushed into a corner. Ramjan Sheikh should no longer be allowed the slightest chance to be alone with the officer. Surely the officer would approve when he discovered in the morning that Akmal Pradhan had stayed the entire night. Despite Kobej's intense reluctance, Pradhan made him stay as well. Ramjan Sheikh didn't like the idea. But he couldn't refuse. He arranged for Akmal Pradhan, Kobej and Ali Akkas to share a room.

They stayed up till very late. At first, Kobej was alarmed by Hawa's terrible screams. Akmal Pradhan and Ali Akkas seemed oblivious. The girl's screams gradually grew fainter and after a while, they couldn't hear her anymore. But Kobej couldn't sleep.

The officer emerged very early the next morning, humming a tune.

By then Ali Akkas, Akmal Pradhan, Ramjan Sheikh and Kobej had settled themselves outside. The officer glanced at them. Then, whistling, he departed from the house. Ramjan Sheikh waited awhile. Then he went to the room where the officer had spent the night. A few minutes later, he emerged with an annoyed expression and said, "That Hares Master has no land or anything. Where are we supposed to bury Hawa Bibi?"

SIX

His night had been sleepless. Now, back home and in his own bed, Kobej still couldn't sleep. His head felt heavy. He knew that this heaviness would dissipate if he could get some sleep. But sleep was elusive—every time he closed his eyes, he felt everything closing in on him. Then he had to scramble to sit up. Still, Kobej tried. Not just so he could get rid of the headache; if he could sleep, he would not feel so restless. Finally, he gave up. But he didn't leave his bed.

Akmal Pradhan had not said a word since they had left Ramjan Sheikh's house that morning. Not even when they were back home. As soon as they had arrived, he had disappeared into his room. But Kobej knew Pradhan would come to him, that he would come soon. He even knew exactly what Pradhan would say when he came. What he didn't know was what he was going to tell Pradhan. He still couldn't decide.

But it was quite clear to him that things were taking an increasingly bad turn. The officer had scolded Akmal Pradhan quite a few times. He had humiliated him. He had made fun of him. All of this had happened right in front of Kobej. He might not have believed it if he had heard about it from someone else. But he had seen it all with his own eyes. It was clear as day to Kobej that the officer lacked the slightest respect for Akmal Pradhan. At the same time Ramjan Sheikh was getting so much attention from the officer. If this went on for a few more days, everyone in the village would conclude that they needn't be afraid of Akmal Pradhan any longer. They would realise that Ramjan Sheikh was the one who mattered, that Akmal Pradhan was nothing.

So no effort was needed to understand why Pradhan wanted Kobej to get rid of Ramjan Sheikh. And Kobej now knew very well that if he didn't do it he would be in trouble as well. Idris was already looking at him belligerently, as if waiting for an excuse to get into a fight. After which he would teach Kobej a lesson. These thoughts made Kobej restless. He would have nowhere to go if Akmal Pradhan became a non-entity. He had to kill Ramjan Sheikh.

But Kobej felt afraid. It was going to be harder now to manage the aftermath of Ramjan Sheikh's murder. If his men found out, they would rip Kobej apart. Just think of Idris. Idris knew that if Ramjan Sheikh was gone, so was he. So if Ramjan Sheikh was killed, Idris would make sure the killer paid dearly. Kobej knew it might well be impossible to deal with all of this.

And Ramjan Sheikh's men weren't his only concern. Now there was the army to fear. Considering the way Ramjan Sheikh seemed to have placed himself in their good graces, if something happened to him, if he was murdered, the army itself would try to find the murderer. And if they succeeded, the last two days had made clear to Kobej what his fate would be. Who knew, they might even skin him alive.

His thoughts made him tremble. Not the thought of the army flaying his skin off his body. He had suddenly recalled Hawa Bibi's face. He shivered when he thought of her—her screams seemed to reach his ears again. Gradually, he grew furious at Ramjan Sheikh. That Sheikh wasn't a human being, and that army officer was even more inhuman. He couldn't understand why the Pakistani officer had done what he

did. Why he had arranged the wedding between the muezzin and Hawa Bibi. And if he did get them married, then why did he keep Hawa Bibi for himself last night? As he wondered about it, Kobej began to think that the officer had played a prank of sorts. He had wanted to deflower Hawa Bibi from the very beginning. What came before that was all a joke, a prank.

These thoughts unsettled Kobej again. He sat up quickly and lit a bidi. He had had no relationship with Hares Master. In fact, Hares Master quite disliked him. Then the man had turned Joy Bangla. But Kobej still didn't understand why Master's mother and sister should have been killed. He himself had carried out several murders. But not a single one had been without cause. The military were killing for no reason. They had set fire to the houses of—and killed everybody related to—the other young men who had left with Hares Master. If they really were so powerful, why didn't they just capture Hares Master and the others? Kobej felt angry. If he had to kill Ramjan Sheikh, if that became necessary, he would kill Ramjan Sheikh. But if he couldn't find Sheikh, would he just go ahead and kill his wife and children, or his parents? Kobej couldn't grasp this strange calculation. Was this how a man behaved?

Meanwhile, Ramjan Sheikh was with the army all the time, agreeing to whatever they said. Akmal Pradhan was behaving in the same manner. They should be trying to talk sense to the military, explain the real situation. But no, they were just applauding whatever action the military was taking. Kobej realised that neither of them really had the guts to try and explain things to the army. If they didn't applaud, they would anger the army. He felt disgust for Ramjan Sheikh and Akmal Pradhan. But he also thought it was a little funny. What had happened to all their bluster? Now, here they were, inviting the officer to dinner, showering him with applause.

Applause, applause! Kobej grew furious again. Why should Ramjan Sheikh and Akmal Pradhan applaud the army? What had they done that deserved such acclaim? And they weren't only applauding. Ramjan Sheikh's eagerness was outstripping the army's. He was the one coming up with various ideas. Akmal Pradhan wanted to do the same thing. Just that Ramjan Sheikh was blocking his access to the military.

Kobej lit another bidi. It would have been better if he could understand all this Joy Bangla, liberated Bangladesh business. If he asked Akmal Pradhan to explain, he would just get a "Be quiet, you won't understand any of this." He had never actually wanted to understand any of it. But now the actions of the army, and

Ramjan Sheikh and Akmal Pradhan's behavior, made him want to understand. By now, he was pretty sure this was serious business. But it also seemed that things weren't exactly the way Akmal Pradhan explained to him sometimes. Nor were they about what the army officer, Ali Akkas and Ramjan Sheikh were always shouting, either. He had seen Hares Master's mother performing her namaz just a few days ago. Kobej knew she said her prayers five times a day. He didn't really understand religion and had never bothered much about it, but he did know what the namaz was and how to perform it. Even if Hares Master had become a Hindu, his mother was still Muslim. Kobej also knew about the other villagers who had been killed. Who among them hadn't performed the namaz? Then why were the officer, Akmal Pradhan and Ramjan Sheikh calling them Hindus? Did this mean that someone could be a Hindu and still do the namaz? Even if that was the case, though, even if they were Hindu, so what? This was what was giving him the most trouble. Even if they had been Hindu, Kobej knew they had never stuck their noses in anybody else's business. Why had they been killed? Kobej didn't understand. All he could think of was that it made no difference if they were Hindu or Muslim—what mattered was whether they had done something wrong or not.

He went back to bed. If only he could get some sleep! But given the rage he was feeling against Ramjan Sheikh and Akmal Pradhan, he knew sleep wouldn't come. Why were Akmal Pradhan and Ramjan Sheikh jumping up and down, shouting Islam-Islam-Pakistan-Pakistan? Didn't Kobej know every skeleton they had in their closets? Hadn't Pradhan once visited a brothel in the city, leaving Kobej to stand guard? Didn't Ramjan Sheikh have the widow Qulsum murdered and her body dumped into the river because she got pregnant with his baby? Kobej knew everything. So, fine, let them do whatever they wanted—visiting brothels and widows—what was it to him? But why did they have to broadcast these lies, why all the big talk? And that son-of-a-bitch army officer—if Kobej could kick that bastard's arse, he would feel so much better. Son of a bitch, if you have a hard-on, why don't you go to a whorehouse!

Kobej awoke just before noon. He couldn't remember when he had finally dozed off. He shook off his lethargy and climbed out of bed. He lit a bidi and pulled on it slowly. If he took a bath now, he would feel as fresh as ever. But before he could leave for a bath, Akmal Pradhan summoned him.

"Were you asleep?" Akmal Pradhan asked.

This was just small talk. He didn't have to respond.

Akmal Pradhan was sitting on his bed. Kobej sat down on the stool beside the bed. Pradhan watched him with a steady gaze. Kobej felt irked. "Why are you looking at me like that?"

"Shall I write out a deed for you?"

"Why would you write out a deed?" Kobej truly didn't understand.

"You don't want the land?" Akmal Pradhan asked with the same fixed gaze. Kobej was silent. "Kobej, you don't understand the situation," Akmal Pradhan practically wailed.

When Kobej still didn't answer, Akmal Pradhan began explaining. Kobej listened with his head bowed. After Pradhan's long speech had ended, he looked up and said he already knew all of this.

Akmal Pradhan looked at him in surprise. After a pause, a smile blossomed on his face and he said it was good that Kobej already knew all this. There was no need to explain everything again in that case. In fact, there had been no need to tell him anything. Pradhan wanted to know when he would get the job done, whether Kobej had decided yet.

Kobej didn't respond to this. After a few moments, he said, "That Ramjan Sheikh isn't a good man."

Akmal Pradhan seemed disappointed. This was exactly what he had been saying all this time. That was why he needed to be done away with.

Kobej mentioned Hawa.

Akmal Pradhan was surprised. "What does Hawa Bibi have to do with any of this?"

"Why did the military kill her?"

Pradhan waved his hand angrily. Why was Kobej raising this issue?

"The military murdered Hawa, but it was also that bastard Sheikh who killed her."

"Let them." Akmal Pradhan was angry. "Let them." Pradhan told Kobej there was no need for him to worry his head about it. Why was he bothering with things he didn't understand?

Kobej smiled. He said the army was quite bad—they were setting houses ablaze, killing people for no good reason. This was how he felt.

Akmal Pradhan looked at him in surprise.

Kobej said, "Ramjan Sheikh is supporting all the bad things the army is doing."

Akmal Pradhan almost pleaded. "Don't say such things, Kobej, don't say such things."

"Why shouldn't I? You're also dancing to the army's tune."

Akmal Pradhan sighed. After a long while he said, "Our country Pakistan . . . "

"Don't tell me this." Kobej shook his head.

Akmal Pradhan sighed again. "I won't. Kobej, just do me this favour. I'll give you two thousand taka. Plus the land."

"Really?"

"Really, my boy."

"Give me some more time to think it over."

Kobej got up before Akmal Pradhan could say anything else. But he understood the whole thing now, there was no need to think it over anymore. He was quite aware what his situation would be if Ramjan Sheikh managed to get full control. The thing was, if Ramjan Sheikh's men found out, they wouldn't let him off. Then there was the fear of the army. Yes, it was fear indeed; his fear of the army was the big thing right now. He had seen for himself, over the past two days, where things stood.

But even apart from this fear, he still did want to think over the business of killing Ramjan Sheikh for a little longer. These days, he had an inkling that losing his head without provocation was harmful. But he still lost it sometimes. Akmal Pradhan had increased the amount he was to be paid. It had become two thousand now. Two thousand taka was a lot of money, and then there was the land. How could he keep his head? Why wouldn't he get all worked up?

He didn't want to be hotheaded, but he couldn't help it. Two thousand taka was more money than he had ever seen in his life. No, actually he *had* seen it, with Akmal Pradhan, but that money hadn't belonged to him. Now Akmal Pradhan wanted to give him two thousand taka. That would be his own. He could spend it any way he wanted. Or he could save it. He would be able to take it out and play with it if he felt like it. Kobej felt that if he demanded it, if he pointed out the risks he would have to take, Akmal Pradhan might raise the amount even further. How far would he go? Another thousand? Why not? And a piece of land too. Even if it was a tiny patch of land, it was still land and it would be his own.

Kobej was in thrall to this dream as he sat down to eat. It wasn't as though getting rid of Ramjan Sheikh would mean nothing but trouble or fearful consequences. There were also some positives to the plan. Yes, at this moment, he could make it seem as if it was the infidels, the Joy Bangla people, who had killed Ramjan Sheikh. Ramjan Sheikh's men or the army might not even suspect Kobej. So maybe he could go ahead. But not right now. Not right now. He reined himself in. A little more, Kobej told himself, let Ramjan Sheikh indulge in excesses just a little more. He patted himself on the back for this sudden insight. Yes, he suspected—or rather, he was certain—that Ramjan Sheikh would employ to increasing levels of cruelty to ingratiate himself even further with the army. The army was going to set many more homes ablaze based on his information. They would certainly shoot many more people dead. And since that son-of-a-swine officer had a whoring habit, Ramjan Sheikh would probably make some effort there as well. Akmal Pradhan would also probably try all sorts of things. But Kobej knew—had seen for himself—that Pradhan would not be able to get anywhere near Ramjan Sheikh. Then who would be the target of everyone's anger? It was an easy calculation, like two plus two equalled four. They would be angry with Ramjan Sheikh. *Then*, Kobej thought with a smile. If he despatched Ramjan Sheikh *then*, everyone would be convinced that it was the Joy Bangla people—folks were also calling them *mukti*—who had killed him.

SEVEN

Akmal Pradhan went out with Kobej later in the evening. Neither of them knew that the Pakistani forces had ventured out for a small foray. Perhaps in play, perhaps without paying undue attention to what they were doing, the troop had found a handful of prey to stuff in their bags. With them was, yes, Ramjan Sheikh. Akmal Pradhan and Kobej received this information when they arrived at the army camp.

Although this was a rather large village, both Akmal Pradhan and Kobej knew those who had been captured. They were, to be honest, faces familiar from everyday encounters. Pradhan and Kobej found out pretty quickly what they had done wrong. It was Idris, Ramjan Sheikh's righthand-man, who told them with relish. Their crime was participating in a Joy Bangla rally with Hares Master about three months ago.

Kobej had not seen them at the rally. But then, they could always attend rallies, or one could say, what if they had attended a rally? People did all kinds of things. Akmal Pradhan had once visited a whorehouse. Ramjan Sheikh had got a widow pregnant and then killed and dumped her body in the river. Idris used to smuggle all kinds of things back and forth across the border even a few days ago. He used to bring back a lot of stuff from India and sell it in the big marketplace at the *ganj*. Why did Idris bring things back from India?

He let Akmal Pradhan know of his mild objection. Akmal Pradhan glared at Kobej. "Why shouldn't they be arrested? Why did they go to the rally?"

"Why aren't they locking up Ramjan Sheikh then?"

"Why would they lock him up?"

"Didn't that bastard invite a Joy Bangla leader to his place for a meal?"

Akmal Pradhan seemed startled when he heard this. He had completely forgotten about it. Kobej was right, although it had happened a while ago. But Pradhan recalled it clearly now. There was some problem at the *ganj* with certain goods that had been smuggled back from India. Ramjan Sheikh had invested a large amount in the consignment. There was a big hullaballoo over those goods, and the police got involved. Sheikh had sought the help of the *ganj* leader at that time. He had paid the leader a hefty amount. The leader had accepted the amount as a "donation for the movement." And one day, he had come by invitation to share a meal at Ramjan Sheikh's house.

Akmal Pradhan's face lit up as he remembered all this. He patted Kobej on the back. He decided immediately that he had to get news of this event to the officer somehow or other. Even thinking about it was making him happy. The whole thing had happened about a year ago, but even back then, the man had already been a Joy Bangla leader. Just a few months ago, in March, he had dropped by the village to deliver a firebrand speech. How would it be if the officer found out about this? Akmal Pradhan pretended to pose the question to himself. It would be wonderful, he told himself, and Ramjan Sheikh would learn a lesson.

But his happiness was brief. He also recalled something else that had happened a year and a half ago. There was a photograph of him too with the Joy Bangla leader. He owned a copy of it, and who knew, maybe the leader also had a copy. Worse, someone else might have a copy. The possibility was negligible. But still, it scared him. He was angry with himself; what had possessed him to get such a photo taken? But what choice had he had then? Of course, he could've *not* done it; it was merely a gesture of sincerity he had wanted to make. Yes, that too had been a financial deal. He had had a special interest, as had the leader, who had taken the initiative to settle the issue when asked. After this, he too had had to make a "donation to the movement." He had been invited to the leader's house for a meal and, on a whim, had arranged for a photograph with the leader.

So he couldn't tell the officer about Ramjan Sheikh. Because then Ramjan Sheikh would tell the officer about him. Did Ramjan Sheikh know about this photo? Akmal Pradhan was frightened. There was no reason for Sheikh to know. But at the very least he did know that once upon a time Akmal Pradhan had enjoyed a very good relationship with the leader. So maybe he did know about the photograph. Would he tell the officer? Akmal Pradhan thought he wouldn't, out of a sense of self-preservation. Both of them had had dealings with the leader because of various business interests. It was better for both to forget all that for the moment.

"He invited the Joy Bangla leader to his house?" With Kobej, he pretended surprise. "Really? I have no memory of this."

Kobej was encouraged by Akmal Pradhan's surprise. He said Pradhan couldn't possibly have forgotten about it already. It was so recent, just the other day . . .

Akmal Pradhan pretended to try to remember. Finally, he nodded. "Oh, yes, I remember now."

"Then why is the military not locking him up?"

"Why should they? So what if he invited that man, he's working for Pakistan now."

"Don't tell me that. Sheikh is just working for himself."

Akmal Pradhan was taken aback at first, but then he grew elated.

"You understand that, my boy? You understand that he's only working for his own benefit?"

"Why wouldn't I understand? He's using Pakistan merely as an excuse."

"But I, Kobej, I *am* working for Pakistan."

Kobej paid no attention to him and instead gazed at the villagers who had been rounded up. Soon, they heard that girls and women of varying ages had also been brought back to camp. Kobej creased his forehead. "Why are they locking up women?"

Akmal Pradhan did not know the answer to that one. He tried to change the subject by turning to watch Ramjan Sheikh, who was moving around busily doing nothing in particular. "Look at that swine, pretending to work."

"Why are the bastards collaring women? Did the women also participate in the protests and rallies?"

Akmal Pradhan gestured to Ramjan Sheikh. "Look at that bastard, showing off. I should probably go over there, Kobej." He quickly made his way to Ramjan Sheikh. Instead of talking to him, Akmal Pradhan stood next to Ali Akkas. He had realised that it would pay off in the future to maintain a good relationship with this man. If he and Ali Akkas joined forces, Ramjan Sheikh wouldn't be able to get his way so easily. Besides, Ali Akkas probably knew about his history with the Joy Bangla leader, the one with whom he had been photographed. It seemed likely. The leader was related to Ali Akkas, they were cousins of some sort. So he should certainly maintain a friendly relationship with Ali Akkas.

Kobej realised that Akmal Pradhan had left in order to avoid him—so that he wouldn't have to answer his questions. He also understood that Akmal Pradhan didn't have much choice other than running away to avoid the questions. What *could* he say? If he tried to respond, he would have to speak against the Pakistani army. Imagine Akmal Pradhan saying something at this moment against the Pakistani army. Kobej laughed to himself. Oh yes, that would be the day. What could he say? He was dying to throw himself at the feet of the army?

But Kobej was angrier with Ramjan Sheikh than he was with Akmal Pradhan. He had been observing him ever since the army had arrived in the village. His eagerness to set houses on fire, to take people away without good reason, seemed boundless. He was the one leading the military to various locations. Kobej realised that the deaths of all the villagers killed that day had benefitted Ramjan Sheikh immensely. In one stroke, he had become owner of a considerable amount of land, besides remaining in the good books of the army.

They had seized several more people that day. They too would surely be killed and their property confiscated by Ramjan Sheikh. Kobej felt that this was why every single member of these families were being killed—so there would be no one left to ever claim the land or the property. He was a fool not to have realised this before. Yes, he nodded to himself, yes, that had to be the reason. The more he thought about it, the more convinced he was. Those who were killed were "guilty" of becoming Hindus. Because a member of their family had joined the Joy Bangla infidels. What sort of reasoning was that?

Kobej tried to gather his thoughts. Suppose Ramjan Sheikh and Akmal Pradhan were right and those who had gone off to join Joy Bangla had indeed become infidels. But how could all their family members suddenly become infidels as well? Was it just because they lived in the same house? When he thought of this, Kobej couldn't suppress his laughter. The sound didn't travel far, but his body kept shaking.

Should he repeat any of this to Ramjan Sheikh or Akmal Pradhan? Should he tell them he had worked it all out—that they were doing all this merely to grab land or other property, that this infidel business was all a sham? Kobej knew he couldn't say it to Ramjan Sheikh. Sheikh would immediately get the army to lock him up on some trumped up charge. He couldn't even say it to Akmal Pradhan. Pradhan would either pretend not to hear, or ask why Kobej was worrying his head trying to understand things he wasn't capable of understanding.

He didn't want to worry his head. But so many things were happening, one after another, right in front of his eyes. They were forcing him to worry. Ramjan Sheikh, Akmal Pradhan, Ali Akkas—he understood why all three had suddenly become so fired up. The closer they managed to get to the army, the more they would benefit, the more power they would have. Akmal Pradhan himself had admitted as much to Kobej. What Kobej couldn't quite understand was why the army was so active. Why were they so busy, why all this shooting, why so many houses set ablaze? Why were they tiring themselves out with cries of "infidels, infidels"?

Kobej thought it was possible that the army was afraid. Fearful people sometimes behaved in this manner. Was the army afraid? Kobej couldn't be certain. But scared people were sometimes in disarray and it seemed to match the army's behaviour. So did that mean the *mukti*, those they had tagged as infidels, were in a strong position right now? Was the army acting this way because they were having trouble bringing them to heel? Kobej was annoyed at himself—how was he supposed to find the answer to these questions? He couldn't ask Ramjan Sheikh, Ali Akkas, or even Akmal Pradhan. He could find out if he could locate someone who was a *mukti*, a Joy Bangla man. But he didn't know any of them. And even if he did, how was he supposed to track them down at this moment?

The bustle around those who had been captured today increased. The prisoners had their hands tied behind their backs and were bound to one another with a separate length of rope. They were unable to shift or move. The first round of torture had already been carried out. Some of the prisoners were still unconscious, lying together in a twisted heap. Many other villagers had arrived at the camp by this time. Almost none of them was here willingly, they had been summoned. Earlier, the officer had made an announcement to the effect that if someone were captured, if the army were holding a trial for him or her, it was mandatory for the villagers to attend. Because, the officer explained, he didn't want to do anything behind closed doors. Whatever he did would be right in front of everyone. Obviously, the officer was not thinking only of himself, he was concerned about the welfare of the villagers as well. If the villagers were present to observe the trial process, it would be beneficial to them in the long run.

Ramjan Sheikh was busy with the prisoners. Akmal Pradhan was helping him. They were untying the prisoners and separating them. Several soldiers surrounded them, but weren't helping with the untying. They weren't interested in these unimportant chores. Kobej could hear Ramjan Sheikh's excited voice from time to time.

He shouted something unintelligible with "Pakistan, Pakistan" interspersed now and then. He kicked a man in the belly. Kobej recognised the man. Roisuddin. He worked on people's fields in exchange for food. It seemed to Kobej that Ramjan Sheikh was particularly angry with Roisuddin because he had no land of his own. Ramjan Sheikh shouted again, but only the word "Pakistan" reached Kobej's ears. The officer sat on a chair a short distance away, his feet resting on a table. A little smile played on his face as he observed the scene. That fucking whoreson and his fucking Pakistan—Kobej turned his eyes away.

Something happened two days later that left the whole village stunned. The Pakistani army had set up a tiny camp on the northern side of the village, at the very edge. Seven soldiers were stationed there constantly as observers. The land beyond the village border grew wilder the farther north one travelled. There was a river—not too wide—across which were trees and scrubland. The ground was uneven, dotted here and there with tall mounds.

On a sudden whim, two soldiers from the northern camp had decided to take a stroll. A long, leisurely, late-afternoon stroll. They ambled quite far from the camp. Suddenly, gunshots rang out. The shots were heard from the village as well. Within minutes, another small group of soldiers armed themselves and set out to discover the source of the shooting. They soon came back with the two soldiers.

They returned to camp with the two dead bodies.

At first, the villagers didn't venture outdoors. No one felt brave enough. They could guess quite well what doomsday awaited them. Perhaps anyone who set foot outside would just be gunned down. Akmal Pradhan and Ramjan Sheikh had the same fear. But they, at least, couldn't afford to stay indoors. That might have even worse consequences. Both of them thought the same thing—maybe they would come under suspicion then. Fearfully, they crept out of their houses.

Spotting them outside, a few other people came out to join them. They moved forward together, like a tiny rally. They stopped for a moment when they were close to the army camp, as if to gather their courage. Approaching the camp had become a scarier proposition. Soldiers were guarding the entire perimeter. They had organised quickly. In the half-light, the soldiers and their firearms looked large and dangerous. For a few moments, the group thought they wouldn't be allowed to go any farther. Akmal Pradhan and Ramjan Sheikh even discussed that possibility briefly. Nothing like that happened. They were able to reach officer. He was standing grimly. The bodies of the two dead soldiers were laid out, on some kind of coarse fabric, next to him.

The entire group looked at the dead soldiers and then hung their heads low, as though they themselves were responsible for those deaths. Akmal Pradhan took a moment to wipe away a tear from the corner of his eye. He was lucky—the officer noticed the gesture. He looked at Akmal Pradhan as if he could feel Pradhan's sympathy deeply.

But the very next moment, it was Akmal Pradhan he attacked. "You see, Pradhan, you Bengalis are basically an ungrateful people. You have no gratitude. You knew, but none of you told me that the Joy Bangla people were busy with anti-state activities so close to us."

Akmal Pradhan wanted to wail and weep when he heard this. But no sound emerged from his throat. Still, he kept repeating, kept swearing in the name of Allah, that he had no idea that the infidels were so close.

The officer looked at him with hard eyes. "You swear in Allah's name?"

Akmal Pradhan nodded vigorously. Yes, he did. He swore in Allah's name.

The officer seemed to smile. "Don't you know Bengalis have no Allah?" At this, Akmal Pradhan's astonishment outstripped his fear.

The officer turned to Ramjan Sheikh. "What do you think, Sheikh?" Ramjan Sheikh didn't know what he could say to appease the officer. "You didn't tell me about these infidels either, Sheikh?"

At once, Ramjan Sheikh also swore by Allah. He said he too had no idea, he hadn't imagined that the Joy Bangla infidels had come so close.

"Why is your imagination so limited, especially since you're locals? I'm surprised." The officer's tone, though, held no surprise. The officer looked at his dead soldiers lying on one side. Then he looked back at them and said, very casually, that he was giving the village twenty-four hours. Yes, twenty-four. If the infidels were not caught by then, if there was no news of the faithless who were responsible for the murders of these two soldiers—who had left the comfort and security of far-off West Pakistan to come here to serve Islam and Pakistan—then not only this village, but every single village surrounding them, every single person they found at the other end of their weapons, would be razed to the ground. No one, not a single human being, would be left alive to witness how dire the consequences of aiding and abetting infidels could be.

A strange silence descended on the area after the officer had finished. After a while, the silence was broken by Ramjan Sheikh. Pausing between words, he said confidently that the infidels, those who were hiding nearby, would definitely be hunted down. They, who were in favour of Pakistan, would track down the infidels who had killed the two soldiers of the great Pakistani army. Only that would be a fitting tribute to these two martyred soldiers.

The officer nodded slightly. "Very well. Twenty-four hours."

Akmal Pradhan rued his delay as they walked home. He had been about to say the same things that Ramjan Sheikh had said—just that he had taken too long to start. He turned to Kobej, smiling a little, and said, "But there's some good news too."

Kobej was surprised. What good news could Akmal Pradhan possibly have found in what had happened? He looked at Akmal Pradhan, who repeated, "Yes, indeed, there's definitely some good news."

"Which is?" Kobej asked.

"Who killed those two soldiers?" Akmal Pradhan's smile was still intact.

Kobej still didn't understand what the good news was. He stared at Akmal Pradhan.

"Why don't you answer? Who killed the soldiers?" Akmal Pradhan asked again.

Perhaps it had been the same people who were called *mukti*. Yes, it had to be them. Who but those freedom fighters would kill Pakistani soldiers? He said as much to Akmal Pradhan.

"Absolutely right." Pradhan seemed very happy. And then he asked what people would say if Kobej killed Ramjan Sheikh now.

That *was* good news. Kobej nodded his head. Yes, good news indeed. He smiled. But to Akmal Pradhan, he said, "You only sing this one song."

"Yes, I do. Kobej, you won't get such a chance again."

Kobej nodded. "I'm thinking of something else, though."

"What?" Akmal Pradhan looked at him through narrowed eyes.

Kobej stared back at Akmal Pradhan, watching him for a few seconds. Why, hadn't Akmal Pradhan realised? The *mukti* fighters had killed those huge, boarlike soldiers. Wasn't that incredible? This was giving Kobej pause.

Akmal Pradhan was annoyed. He said in a heavy voice, "You won't get another chance like this, Kobej."

Kobej didn't respond. Instead he said, "Ramjan Sheikh said he would capture the *mukti* in twenty-four hours. How is he going to find them? The army is going to shove a bamboo pole right up his arse."

EIGHT

However, that didn't happen. Nothing bad happened either. For instance, the village was not set on fire, people were not lined up and shot. Instead, two young *mukti* fighters were caught. And it was Ramjan Sheikh who could claim most of the credit. Ramjan Sheikh had had some idea about where the *mukti bahini* could be hiding, where they could take shelter if they did arrive in this area. He started off bright and early, leading a large group of soldiers. In the meantime, after the news had reached the *ganj*, a second troop of soldiers had arrived. They remained in the village. The officer accompanied the troop that went with Ramjan Sheikh. Early in the evening, with about two hours left of the twenty-four hour deadline, the group returned. With them were two young freedom fighters. Ramjan Sheikh looked tired but his face was shining with joy.

The whole village poured out to watch. Sheikh grew even more eager and busy now that he had an audience. He turned around suddenly and kicked the two *mukti* fighters to the ground. But this evoked no response among the villagers.

Several poles had been thrust into the ground in front of the camp.

The freedom fighters were tied to two of them. The soldiers came and went as they pleased, freely slapping, kicking and punching the young men. The trial was to be held later, the next morning. This would continue till then. The villagers had also been granted the right to slap them around. But they didn't seem very keen. Their interest seemed to lie elsewhere. They gazed at the boys in astonishment.

Kobej was feeling the same way. He couldn't take his eyes off the two young men. Finally, he asked Akmal Pradhan, "These two killed those soldiers?"

Akmal Pradhan nodded. These two, or perhaps others from their group. But most probably these two—surely the military wouldn't catch the wrong ones.

These two? These two! Kobej couldn't quite believe it. "But they're only boys!" How could they have killed those giant soldiers!

"Only boys?" Akmal Pradhan pretended to be irked. "They're snakes!" He wasn't particularly interested in this conversation right now. Ramjan Sheikh had indeed succeeded in catching the freedom fighters—this thought had taken over his mind. He could guess quite clearly what was about to happen. The *ganj* Peace Committee leader Ali Akkas wasn't here. He had taken off to make speeches in various places. If he was around Akmal Pradhan could have indirectly asked for some guidance. He was close to losing his faith in Kobej. Why did Kobej not understand that it was he who would be at a disadvantage if things continued this way? What more could Akmal Pradhan do to explain the situation? He had done enough, said enough. He was ready to hand over two thousand taka, and write him a piece of land, too. What else did Kobej want? More money? Then why didn't he come out and say so?

Kobej said, "How did these two kill those soldiers?"

"The same thing, over and over again!" Akmal Pradhan scolded Kobej.

Kobej shut up, but didn't abandon his thoughts. He couldn't accept that these two young men had killed the soldiers. He couldn't tear his eyes away from the two figures bound to the poles. He also wondered what made these youngsters fight against the army. Were they infidels too? Kobej looked at them sharply. The last few days had given him an idea of what an infidel or kafir could be like. But these two didn't seem to fit. "The bastards, labelling everyone an infidel. The bastards, checking to see whether others have their heads covered while their own naked arses are open to the wind." Kobej nodded slightly as he gazed at the young men. They had certainly pulled off something big by killing the soldiers. And why shouldn't they? If the military could just brand anyone they wanted an "infidel" and kill them, why shouldn't they retaliate by killing the army? Kobej felt this was only right. He could even say as much to Akmal Pradhan. Yes, why not, he could even say it to Ramjan Sheikh. He looked up again. There was a crowd gathered next to the young men; Ramjan Sheikh was there as well, busy. There was no time. Kobej knew he was running out of time, he had to take a decision about Ramjan Sheikh quickly. Any day now, Akmal Pradhan would say, fine, you don't have to do the job. I'm not giving you any money or land. Kobej chuckled. He knew Akmal Pradhan wasn't going to say any such thing. And anyway, he had almost decided on the Ramjan Sheikh question. He looked at the crowd again. He watched as Ramjan Sheikh kicked one of the young men on the hips again. Kobej looked away. The decision was taken. All that remained was to turn it into action.

It had been announced yesterday that none of the villagers were allowed to stay indoors today. The order had resulted in a growing crowd since early this morning. Ramjan Sheikh had made arrangements for the villagers to sit or stand in front of the primary school. He was dressed in a new *panjabi* today. And a new skullcap, on which the words "Pakistan *Zindabad*," written in Arabic script, were embroidered in gold thread.

Obviously, Akmal Pradhan was there with Kobej too. But today, he wasn't standing next to Kobej. He had gone straight to the officer. He would compete with Ramjan Sheikh in performing various tasks today, no matter what the officer said. He had also instructed Kobej to be busy like Idris, even if a little, instead of just standing around. It would only benefit Kobej if he caught the officer's attention.

But Kobej stood by himself to one side. He was trying to catch sight of the two *mukti* boys. There was a crowd in front of them: several Pakistani soldiers, the officer, Akmal Pradhan, Ramjan Sheikh and Idris. The primary leader of the local Peace Committee, Ali Akkas, wasn't present. But a few of his men were, as was his son Shafiqur. They and a few other young men had the *mukti* boys more or less surrounded. Kobej could still make out, even from what little he could see, that the two had suffered greatly the previous night. Even now, the soldiers were kicking the two boys, hitting them with guns, at their pleasure.

Kobej moved forward step by step. He noticed that no matter how hard they were hit, not a single sound escaped their lips. Their noses and lips were split, there was blood in the corners of their eyes. Their bodies were positioned awkwardly because they were tied to the poles with their hands behind their backs. But, to Kobej, they looked like lion cubs. Ready to pounce as soon as they were set loose.

The trial began. First, Ramjan Sheikh made a speech. Today, he seemed unable to gather his thoughts coherently. He kept repeating himself. He praised the Pakistani army unreservedly and warned all those present to beware of Indian infidels. He also informed everyone that, pretty soon, they would see an example of the consequences of siding with, or aiding, the infidels.

After Ramjan Sheikh was done, Akmal Pradhan got the chance to speak. It happened quite suddenly. No one knew what was supposed to happen after Sheikh's speech. Then the officer gestured at Akmal Pradhan. "Would you like to say something, Pradhan? Yes?" At first, Akmal Pradhan couldn't believe it. Like a fool, he kept silent. The officer laughed. "So you have nothing to say, Pradhan, right?"

Who said he had nothing to say? Who could even imagine such a thing? Akmal Pradhan practically ran to the spot Ramjan Sheikh had just vacated. He glanced at the officer, at the gathered villagers, at Kobej, and, out of the corner of his eye, at Ramjan Sheikh. Then he began to speak. He was eloquent. The villagers concentrated on his every word, while Ramjan Sheikh stared through narrowed eyes and the officer looked on, smiling thinly.

When Pradhan finished his speech, the officer called him near.

"Good, you've spoken well. Now stay here beside me." Pradhan bared his teeth in a silent smile. He placed himself on one side of the officer.

Ramjan Sheikh stood on the other.

The trial itself didn't last long. The officer, with Pradhan and Sheikh on either side, tried to get the young men to talk. The same attempt had been made last night. Neither of them had said a word. Even now, though almost dead from the torture they had endured through the night, they wouldn't admit anything. The officer beckoned to a burly soldier. He grasped the arm of one of the boys, and with an odd twist, broke it. The boy writhed. The villagers heard the sound of his bones cracking. But not even the smallest of sounds escaped his lips. The second boy's arm was broken in the same manner. A murmur went through the villagers. But they turned to stone when the officer swivelled around to look at them. The officer, flanked by Akmal Pradhan and Ramjan Sheikh, went up to the young men and kicked them. Ramjan Sheikh followed suit, while Akmal Pradhan slapped one of them. But the attempt to wrest information failed this time as well. Their bodies drooped against the stakes, but they didn't make a sound.

They were hit by another wave of torture.

When this attempt failed too, the officer tried to entice them with the promise of freedom. This bait had been dangled several times last night as well. Now, when the officer tried to lure them again, in everyone's presence, one of the young men spat in his face. Insulted and enraged, the officer retreated with his fist raised. Three or four brawny soldiers with guns moved towards the young men. The burly soldiers used brute strength as well as the butts of their rifles. The young men became unrecognisable within minutes. Nothing was left of them, no eyes, no noses, no mouths. Their bodies were ripped to bits.

Ramjan Sheikh had a brainwave. He explained something to the officer, smiling. A subtle smile appeared on the officer's lips. He nodded. Sheikh called Idris over and gave him instructions. Soon Idris, along with a few more of Sheikh's goons, became very busy. They fetched a pair of tall bamboo poles. The remnants of the two young men were tied to the poles with ropes. Then the poles were raised and set into the ground. Akmal Pradhan lent a hand. Ramjan Sheikh explained that this would be useful in the long run. Any infidels in the surrounding villages would take to their heels when they realised what their fate would be.

The officer patted Ramjan Sheikh on the back lightly.

Akmal Pradhan looked happy on the way home. He wasn't despondent like he used to be, although Ramjan Sheikh had outdone him in the end and the officer had patted him on the back. He was happy—the officer had given him a place by his side. Now if he could just get Ramjan Sheikh out of the picture, his own place was assured.

He looked at Kobej with a smile and asked how his speech had gone down.

Kobej nodded but didn't say anything.

Akmal Pradhan asked whether Kobej had noticed something.

Kobej had no desire to talk or listen right now. But he looked at Pradhan.

Although there was no need to, Pradhan lowered his voice. He said now was the best time to get rid of Ramjan Sheikh. If something happened to Sheikh now, everyone would think it was the *mukti bahini*.

Yes, that was true, Kobej nodded. Ramjan Sheikh had just got two *mukti* fighters killed. They were so young, practically children. And Kobej still couldn't quite understand what crime they had committed. Akmal Pradhan scolded him. How would Kobej understand what crimes those infidels had committed? Pakistan, Bangladesh, India—did Kobej even understand any of this?

Kobej shook his head. No, he didn't. But even if he didn't, there was one thing he did understand. Whatever the *mukti* were doing had to be right—they were passionate about it.

Akmal Pradhan was extremely surprised. What was Kobej talking about? What was all this nonsense?

Not nonsense at all, laughed Kobej. He was right. How could the *mukti* bear all that torture if they weren't so committed to their cause?

Akmal Pradhan clamped his hand on Kobej's mouth. "Shut up, you fool!" He warned Kobej that he would be dead if Ramjan Sheikh or the officer were to hear any of this. He must forget this, he must forget all this nonsense. Akmal Pradhan paused and stroked Kobej's back. Kobej should only think about Ramjan Sheikh now.

Think of Ramjan Sheikh? Kobej laughed. Ramjan Sheikh, who had killed those children and then strung them up on bamboo poles . . .

What was the point in talking about all this? Akmal Pradhan spoke indulgently. He was going to give Kobej two thousand taka, some land too. Why didn't Kobej think about the money and the land?

Kobej was quiet.

"Why don't you say something, Kobej?" Akmal Pradhan felt impatient. "I'm telling you, Kobej, you won't get another chance like this. Why don't you talk, Kobej?"

"Thinking. I'm thinking."

NINE

Kobej woke Akmal Pradhan in the middle of the night. His clothes were blood-spattered, hair dishevelled and eyes bloodshot. He practically shoved Akmal Pradhan. "I finished him. I got rid of him."

"Whom, Kobej? Whom did you finish?"

"Ramjan Sheikh is no more in this world."

"He's not?" Akmal Pradhan's voice cracked with joy. "Are you telling the truth, Kobej?" "I slit his throat." Pradhan jumped up. "I'll give you money, Kobej. Shall I write some

land over to you? Just tell me, Kobej, what is it you want? Money, land . . . "

Kobej smiled. He rummaged through his pockets, pulled out a bidi and lit it. He seemed impossibly calm and composed. He looked at Akmal Pradhan, took one step towards him.

"Why are you looking at me like that, Kobej?" Pradhan was suddenly afraid. Kobej smiled again. In a surprisingly cool, detached tone, he said, "What can *you* give me, Pradhan, what can you give? I didn't kill him for the money."

Interregnum

Kobej returned to the village on December 15, 1971. He didn't return alone; he came back with a huge group of freedom fighters. Hares Master was in the group, as was another man from the village.

He had crossed the border into India after murdering Ramjan Sheikh and his failed attempt at murdering Akmal Pradhan. He spent a month on the other side, doing odd jobs. He didn't know what to do now, how he should proceed. Then he ran into Hares Master. Hares Master was astonished to see him. He couldn't understand what Kobej was doing there, on the other side of the border. "Kobej, why are you here?"

"I want to join the *mukti bahini*," Kobej replied.

Hares Master was even more surprised. He had never had a good relationship with Kobej. But he knew what kind of man Kobej was and whose man he was.

"*You* want to join the freedom fighters?"

"I do. Didn't I just slit open Ramjan Sheikh's throat?"

Some news from the village always reached Hares Master, even in exile. And he knew who Ramjan Sheikh was. Still, he asked Kobej why he had slaughtered Sheikh.

Kobej couldn't coherently explain why. But he had indeed slaughtered Sheikh.

Hares Master believed him. He understood a good deal from Kobej's account. But he waited a couple of weeks to be certain about him. Then he spoke to his troop leader and got Kobej in.

Kobej was ecstatic. He said he had killed Ramjan Sheikh, yes, but Akmal Pradhan had escaped. "He needs to be killed too."

Hares Master laughed. "Not just him. Every single person who's aiding the Pakistani army needs to be killed."

Now, on his return to the village on December 15, 1971, Kobej couldn't wait to get Akmal Pradhan. He had by then made a name for himself as a freedom fighter. He had performed some of the most dangerous tasks during operations undertaken by the group, sometimes even getting into trouble for taking too many risks. Their troop leader had told them repeatedly, war didn't always mean advancing—sometimes it meant retreat too. Kobej had never liked that. But his troop had never faced danger because of him. Rather, his name had spread from mouth to mouth.

Hares Master stopped him from rushing to Akmal Pradhan's house.

They already knew that Pradhan wasn't there—he had fled. Some of their troops had already visited Pradhan's house. Kobej didn't know because he and his group had arrived a few hours later. Kobej chuckled.

"He's fled? Where can he fly to? I'll find him."

Hares Master paid no attention to Kobej. He was miserable. He had already heard of his mother and sister's fate from Kobej. Now that he was back in the village, he could barely contain himself as their memories flooded him. He wasn't crying, though. He had told himself that men didn't cry, it didn't suit them. Besides, this was a time for restraint. This village, many neighbouring villages, indeed, a large swathe of Bangladesh had already been liberated. But there were regions where the Pakistani army still continued to resist. Even their nearest town was still under Pakistani control.

If he began weeping, many members of the small troop he had led into the village would begin crying too. The whole group would fall apart. There was still a war to be fought—he couldn't break down and compromise his troops now.

But they didn't have to fight anymore. The Pakistani army surrendered the very next day. The country had been liberated. Hares Master asked Kobej with a smile, "We did it, Kobej, we liberated the country! What does liberation mean, Kobej?"

Kobej shook his head vigorously. No, he didn't know all that. Nor did he want to know.

Hares laughed and asked why he didn't want to know. How could he not want to know!

Still Kobej demurred. "No, I don't. You're going to say complicated things. I'm not listening to any of it."

Hares Master laughed again. So Kobej didn't need to understand why the country was liberated?

Kobej shook his head. No, there was no need for him to understand. Whether he understood or not, the country had been liberated. He didn't want to hear difficult explanations and get his head in a twist.

"All right then," said Hares Master. He wouldn't try to explain anything to Kobej. Kobej could work it out for himself, in whatever way he wanted. It was probably better if he slowly gained that understanding on his own.

Their camp was disbanded a few days later. Not everyone in their group was from this village and one by one, they dispersed. Only three of them, Kobej, Hares and another man, were from hereabouts. None of them had a place to live. Kobej had never had it anyway, and Hares Master's home had been razed to the ground, as had the house of the third man, Ismail. Another young man had gone off to war with Hares Master—he had not made it back.

The day after the camp was dissolved, Kobej accosted Hares Master. They could probably find food and shelter for a few days more. Most households in the village had opened their doors to the freedom fighters. But this was no way to live. Hares Master didn't have enough money to rebuild his house for the three of them—himself, Kobej and Ismail—to live in. Kobej told him, "Why don't you just take over Ramjan Sheikh's house? I can take Akmal Pradhan's, and Ismail can stay with me."

Hares Master was about to get angry, but laughed instead. "What are you saying, Kobej?"

"What do you think I'm saying? Don't we have to live?"

"Does Sheikh's house belong to us? Does Pradhan's?"

So what, Kobej said. He knew those houses didn't belong to them. But Akmal Pradhan and Ramjan Sheikh had supported

Pakistan. And they had fought against Pakistan. Now they had nowhere to live. They could take over those two houses.

No, they couldn't, said Hares Master. They couldn't just occupy other people's property. So, Kobej wanted to know, what was going to happen to those two houses?

Hares Master himself wasn't sure. Never mind Ramjan Sheikh's house—Sheikh was dead, and there was no news of his family. Akmal Pradhan's family had vanished, as had Akmal Pradhan himself. But Hares Master had no idea whether he was dead or alive, or where he might be. He thought it over for a few minutes and told Kobej that the government would decide about the houses.

"Why should the government get them?" Kobej asked.

"Of course the government should take the houses. Not us."

"Then what will happen to us?" Kobej asked. "Will the government build us houses?"

Such a thought had vaguely occurred to Hares Master as well. He had no money at hand, nor did he have any savings. If only the government would make some arrangement to provide them with a roof over their heads. He didn't mention this to Kobej, however. Instead, he yelled, "Why should the government build us a house? We'll build our own."

Kobej laughed at this. "Hah! No rice in our bellies, no clothes to cover our arses, but look at us! Building houses!"

He told Hares he would wait and see a few days longer. If nothing came through by then, he would claim Akmal Pradhan's house for himself.

A few days later, there was a commotion in the village. A car full of men had arrived from the *ganj*. They went straight to

Ramjan Sheikh's house and took over the place. One of them, a man who was always surrounded by several others, summoned Hares Master.

Kobej showed up along with Hares Master. The man seemed happy to see him. "Ah, so this is Kobej!" Yes, yes, he had heard of Kobej. It was because of fighters like him that the country had been liberated so quickly! The man praised Hares Master as well. He praised both of them. Repeatedly. He said that the nation and the people would always remember them.

A slight smile blossomed on Hares Master's lips. Kobej was silent.

He couldn't work out who this flamboyant man was. Or why he was here all of a sudden, making speeches. Of course the man had not arrived at the village without a reason.

That became clear soon. But first, he turned to Kobej. "People say you killed Ramjan Sheikh. Is that true?"

"Yes, it is," said Hares Master before Kobej could reply.

But the man wanted to hear it from Kobej. "Let him talk."

Kobej said, yes, he was the one who had got rid of Ramjan Sheikh.

The man smiled. "Good work, Kobej."

Kobej already knew this. He had no need to hear it from others. He didn't like the man's behaviour one bit. He turned to Hares Master, who was sitting beside him, and asked in a low voice who the man was. The man overheard him. His face was suffused with a lovely smile. He gazed at Kobej as if he was enjoying Kobej's naiveté and wasn't irked by the fact that Kobej did not know who he was or recognise him. He raised a hand to stop Hares Master. "Let me tell him."

He turned back to Kobej and smiled. "You understand, Kobej, I'm your leader."

Leader! Kobej stared dumbfounded. What was this man a leader of? Kobej wanted to know. The leader's smile didn't disappear. Why, hadn't Kobej just fought in the war of liberation? Kobej should know, he was the local leader during the war.

"Hares Master is my leader," said Kobej.

"Yes, yes, that is true." However, Hares was leader of a small group. He was leader of a bigger group. He was not only Kobej's leader, he was Hares Master's leader as well.

"Where were you?" Kobej asked with narrowed eyes.

The leader didn't understand Kobej's question.

Kobej clarified that he was trying to ascertain where exactly the leader had been during the war.

The leader smiled again. "I was around," he said briefly.

"I didn't see you."

The leader said, as if explaining to a child, "Is it possible to see every single person? Is it even necessary? If everyone just fought, who would do the other work?" He had been elsewhere, doing other things.

"I understand. You don't have to say more," Kobej said with the hint of a smile.

The leader grew serious. "What are you saying, Kobej? What is it you understand?"

"You were doing other things."

The smile didn't return to the leader's face. Grimly, he turned to Hares Master. He was in a hurry so he would quickly say his piece and leave. He even listed all the important places he had to visit. Since Ramjan Sheikh was dead and there was no information on the whereabouts of his family, something should be done about his house, he said.

"What?" Hares Master asked eagerly.

The leader replied that to avoid controversy, he would keep the house directly under his control for now. When the government came to a decision, they would reassess the situation. Of course he was a representative of the government, so the house being under his control was tantamount to the house being under government control. He, of course, had no interest in taking on this responsibility. But because there were so many conflicts over the possession of such abandoned houses, he was forced to take this on despite his reluctance.

And Akmal Pradhan's house, what about that one? Neither Kobej nor Hares Master actually asked that question, but the leader seemed to divine it from their faces. He reassured them, "A decision has certainly been made regarding Akmal Pradhan's house."

Several freedom fighters, educated men from the *ganj*, had decided they wanted to establish a sort of club-house there. The club would be responsible for providing entertainment for the villagers. They would also provide some social services. The club wasn't going to be a permanent entity—it would exist only until the government decided what to do with Akmal Pradhan's house. If, later on, the villagers decided that they needed the club in the village, they could apply to the government.

Kobej was furious when he heard this. Hares Master's brows creased. Who were these educated freedom fighters from the *ganj* opening this club at Akmal Pradhan's house? He knew all the freedom fighters from this region. "Of course, of course," the leader said. Hares Master must know them all. For instance, surely he knew Shafiqur.

No, Hares Master didn't know him. He stared at the leader.

"*Arre*, Shafiqur, Shafiqur," said the leader. "You don't know him? He's my nephew."

Hares Master recognised him then. So did Kobej. Shafiqur was Ali Akkas's son.

But when had Shafiqur joined the freedom fighters? Kobej had seen him visit the village even around June or July last year. If Shafiqur had indeed joined the *mukti bahini*, how would he have been able to visit the Pakistani army at that time? Kobej, however, didn't express his doubts. Who knew, there might be some inside information he wasn't privy to. He expressed anxiety over the fate of the two houses. "Are you taking over those two houses then?"

The leader was vexed. Hadn't he already made clear that this was only a temporary arrangement until the government came to a decision? This was being done so that the houses were not grabbed by someone. He explained all this to Kobej in a serious voice.

"But then where are we supposed to live?" Kobej asked, also in a serious voice.

"Why? Don't you have a place to live?" The leader seemed surprised. Hares explained their situation to him. The leader made sympathetic "aha aha" noises. "Our independence is built on the sacrifices of so many people! It is only because people made

133

these sacrifices that liberation came." The leader's epiphany, how-ever, did not resolve the issue of their lack of housing. Kobej made a proposal. Fine, the leader could take charge of Ramjan Sheikh's house. Let him hand Akmal Pradhan's house over to them. Hares Master, Ismail and Kobej could live there together. His proposal was rejected immediately. The leader said, "No, no, how can that be? The boys have their fancies too. Anyway, they're only setting up this club for the benefit of the village."

"Then tell the government. Let them build a house for us."

The leader grew sombre again. He expressed sadness at Kobej's outburst. But he tried to explain the situation to him. The country had been liberated just a few weeks ago. The land had been ravaged by war. Now was the time to rebuild. This was not something the government could accomplish by itself. Every-one would have to step forward and pitch in. It was another war they had to fight. The government couldn't possibly build houses for everyone. Everyone had suffered some damage. Was it possible for the government to remedy all of it? It was inappropriate to even say such a thing.

"Then who is going to make arrangements for me?" Kobej asked.

The leader didn't have an answer to that. He smiled and tried to shrug it off. One of his companions whispered in his ear and he nodded immediately. As though he wanted to say, "Of course! Of course!" He smiled sweetly at Kobej. "I will look into it. Of course I will. Today, or tomorrow at the latest, I will write to the government to inform them of the situation here. I'm sure some arrangement will be made."

That very afternoon a group of men came and settled into the houses of Ramjan Sheikh and Akmal Pradhan. Hares Master knew almost every single one of them. The leader belonged to a large family—these men were all related to him in some way. There was a handful of outsiders as well. One of them was a surprise. Entaz, a member of the group setting up in Akmal Pradhan's house, was a well-known pickpocket who usually operated in and around the *ganj* cinema halls. He was also in the business of defrauding village bumpkins visiting the *ganj*.

Although Hares Master was merely surprised, Kobej was furious. He blamed Hares for the whole mess. None of this would have happened if Hares had taken his advice. He had told Hares to take over Ramjan Sheikh's house at the very beginning and he and Ismail could have shared Akmal Pradhan's. But Hares had paid no attention. Look what had happened now. Hares laughed. How could he just take over Ramjan Sheikh's house? How could he let Kobej occupy Akmal Pradhan's house? Neither of the houses belonged to them.

"It's all very well to tell us all this, but you couldn't stop them, could you?"

Hares Master stammered a response. They hadn't been taken over—the leader had said that this was only until the government made a decision about the houses.

"Don't tell me all this anymore." Kobej grew angry. No one would be able to oust the leader and his men from those two houses now. He couldn't be fobbed off with lies anymore. He understood a lot now.

Kobej ignored Hares when he began protesting. "I'm not ready to hear anything. You have to make some sort of arrangement for me."

"I'm sure there will be some arrangement," Hares said.

But Kobej was adamant that Hares be the one to do it.

"Why are you angry with me?"

"Why did you let go of those houses?"

Hares Master was quiet.

Kobej said he didn't know anyone else and didn't want to know anyone else. He knew Hares Master. Hares Master had been his leader during the war. So he was the one who would have to organise something for Kobej.

A few days later, he confronted Hares again. He wanted to know whether Hares knew Shafiqur. Kobej had some doubts about Shafiqur, who had visited the village in 1971 with Ali Akkas. Hares Master's forehead furrowed. "Why didn't you tell me this before?"

"What difference would it have made?" Kobej responded angrily, but also told him he had picked up some news at the *ganj*. Apparently, Shafiqur had remained there throughout the war. He had passed the war eating, drinking and watching films. Then, in mid-December, he was suddenly a *mukti*. He even had arms. The *ganj* people were laughing about it. But no one had the guts to say anything, because he was the leader's nephew. He also had a large group of followers of his own. And he had weapons at his disposal. Even if they were merely weapons left behind by the Pakistani army, all weapons fired bullets.

Kobej reported all of this to Hares and asked what he should do.

"Is it all true, what you're saying?" Hares Master asked in a sombre voice.

"It's not just me! Everyone's talking about it."

"Everyone . . ." Hares Master didn't finish.

"Why don't you say something? What are you going to do to him?"

Hares Master was silent.

"Inform the police. Let them tie him up and give him a good walloping."

Hares Master smiled.

Kobej grew enraged again. He didn't like any of this. If Shafiqur was a *mukti*, then Ramjan Sheikh and Akmal Pradhan were freedom fighters as well. Shafiqur and his gang had set up a club at Akmal Pradhan's house. Which meant Akmal Pradhan still had control over the house. Hares Master was to blame for all of this. He refused to hear anything Kobej was telling him. Nor was he paying any attention to Kobej's comfort. Then why had he been Kobej's leader during the war?

Shafiqur had a firearm. And Kobej had surrendered his own because Hares had told him to. He had wanted to keep one or two nice guns for himself. But Hares hadn't let him keep a single one. So he should now make sure that Shafiqur surrendered his weapons as well.

Hares grew a little upset with Kobej. "You're overdoing it, Kobej. So what if Shafiqur has a gun?"

"Why should he? If I don't have one, why should he?"

Hares didn't understand why this was bothering Kobej so much. Kobej repeated himself. Why was Hares not getting it? It was a problem—Shafiqur had a gun and Kobej didn't. Why was it so hard for Hares to understand this simple problem?

"But you *shouldn't* have a firearm," Hares explained. The government asked everyone to surrender their weapons, the freedom fighters complied and that was that. A crooked smile appeared on Kobej's face. "Then how come Shafiqur has a gun?" He threw out the question and watched Hares with sharp eyes. "Shafiqur wasn't even a *mukti*. He shouldn't even have a gun. But he does. So you're saying the freedom fighters should surrender their weapons, but those who are pretending to be *mukti* now that the war is over should be allowed to keep theirs?"

Hares Master had no answer.

"Do you know the things Shafiqur does, jamming his gun against people's chests?"

Hares Master gave no answer.

"You just go silent whenever I say something."

"Why are you telling me all this?" Hares Master tried to sound angry. "What am I supposed to do?"

"Who else am I supposed to tell?" Kobej asked, astonished. But the next moment, he was angry again. He didn't care for Shafiqur's behavior at all, not one bit. Kobej was liable to cross swords with him any day now. He wanted to. He was only looking for a chance. But he couldn't just start a fight. Let Shafiqur give him that chance. He'd then teach Shafiqur a lesson.

But if he was at a disadvantage because he didn't have a weapon on him, Hares Master would be to blame. Kobej made himself clear on this.

Somehow or other, Hares Master managed to construct two rooms. So they no longer had to spend their nights elsewhere. Master, Kobej and Ismail began living together. But money was scarce. The *ganj* leader had come by again and officially reopened the school. But everything was in disarray. There was no assurance that next month's wages would arrive. The leader had mentioned that those who had participated in the war would get some kind of pension, but everything was still uncertain.

It was this uncertainty that made Kobej angrier. Three people needed a considerable amount to live on. Hares was making do somehow. But this arrangement wasn't to Kobej's liking either. He told Hares this couldn't go on. Hares didn't want to take him seriously. "Why are you getting so anxious, Kobej?" They were getting by somehow, weren't they?

Kobej shook his head. This wasn't right. He was a free man. He wanted to live as he saw fit. He was ashamed to live off of Hares Master day after day. And it wasn't just him. Hares must be finding it difficult too. He wanted an independent existence. "I don't like this anymore. No rice in the belly, nothing to cover the arse. Make some other arrangement for me, you hear?"

What arrangement could Hares make? He knew quite well that they couldn't go on like this. But what choice did they have? Although there was a plan he was considering. Not only for Kobej, but for many others in the village. Between the two of them, Akmal Pradhan and Ramjan Sheikh had owned quite a substantial amount of land. They could use all this land and start a farming cooperative. First, they had to form a collective. Those who had suffered damage during the war, those who caused no one offence, those who were poor and landless—they could all join forces to farm that land. They would share the labour as well as the harvest. It would be fruitful for everyone involved and benefit the nation too.

But planning alone didn't make it real. All sorts of obstacles had to be overcome. There were so many people just waiting to put a spanner in the works. He should also find out if the collective was a good idea for this land in the first place. He decided to talk it over with the *ganj* leader in a few days. They would move ahead as soon as they received approval.

This was what he told Kobej. Kobej seemed slightly happier when he heard of the plan. But he was furious the moment he was told about discussions with the *ganj* leader. "Why? You tell me: why do you need to discuss any of this with that son of a bitch?"

Hares laughed at Kobej's rage. "You won't understand, Kobej."

Kobej grew angrier. "Akmal Pradhan used to say the same thing to me—you won't understand. So do you. Why won't I understand? Explain to me, why won't I understand?"

Hares Master tried, but the smile didn't quite materialise. In a tired voice he said, "Who will explain to *me*, Kobej? Do I understand any of it?"

Things did not improve. Hares Master received no wages at the end of the month. It wasn't just him, everyone at the school was in the same situation. Not all the students had paid their dues and the rich people hadn't made enough donations. So the schoolteachers were not going to get paid. The school was partly funded by student dues, the shortfall being made up from the charity of rich villagers and *ganj* folks. In the past, both Ramjan Sheikh and Akmal Pradhan used to make gifts to the school. Sometimes hefty grants were available from the government or other large institutions.

Now the students could no longer pay their dues. Ramjan Sheikh was gone and so was Akmal Pradhan. The *ganj* leader had made promises but failed to obtain any governmental help. So no wages for the teachers. Hares Master's face grew long. Kobej laughed when he saw. "How does it feel? Now that you have no wages, how does it feel?"

"How should it feel?" Hares Master was angry. "Do I have to describe how it feels?"

Hares's anger didn't touch Kobej. "What do you, mean do you have to describe it? My heart wants to know!"

Hares Master was so angry he couldn't speak.

Kobej changed the subject. He asked if Hares knew how long it would take for the government to make a decision.

"What decision?" The government was having to make all kinds of decisions these days. Hares stared at Kobej.

"You know, about Ramjan Sheikh and Akmal Pradhan's houses." It had been ages since the leader had talked about them. Since then, nothing.

"I don't know," Hares shook his head.

"You don't know anything."

Hares was annoyed. How could he know? How was he supposed to know what the government was up to?

"Why aren't you in the government?" Kobej asked.

"Me? Why would I . . . *how* could I be in the government? I don't belong to the government party, do I?"

Pretending not to understand, Kobej said, "Why shouldn't you be in the government? You fought in the war." He grew angry as he spoke.

"How can that man at the *ganj* be the leader? He didn't even fight." Kobej hadn't seen him anywhere. Not on the battlefields, nor anywhere else.

Hares Master smiled. Why was Kobej getting so angry? The leader had told them that even if he hadn't fought, he had been busy elsewhere.

"Where was he busy? In a whorehouse?"

Hares Master objected. Why was Kobej making these loud allegations? Did he have any proof?

"You're the one who told me."

"When did I tell you something like that?" Hares Master couldn't recall.

Kobej reminded him. Hares had indeed said as much once. But not recently—it was when the war was still raging. And he hadn't said it about the *ganj* leader in particular. He had merely said that there were many people like them who were fighting this war on an empty stomach, while some leaders were busy with women and wine.

Hares Master nodded. Yes, he had said that. But that had been about a handful of leaders. Not everyone had behaved that way. If all the leaders had behaved so badly, why, the country would never have been liberated.

Kobej said solemnly, "That might be true. But I know for sure that the *ganj* leader is one of the bad ones."

"How do you know?"

"Don't you see how he took over those two houses? And now he's not letting go of them."

"He will, he will," Master said. "As soon as the government arrives at a decision . . . "

Kobej lost his temper again. "Don't tell me that. He's turned Shafiqur into a *mukti* . . . "

Why should that matter to Kobej? Let Shafiqur pretend to be a freedom fighter, it made no difference to Hares Master or Kobej.

Kobej stared at him in outrage. What was Hares saying! No, that wasn't what he thought at all. It did make a difference to him that Shafiqur was pretending to be a freedom fighter. Kobej didn't care if Shafiqur suddenly became very rich, if he bought up all the land around them, if he became a big leader. But it bothered him when Shafiqur played at being a *mukti*. Why didn't it bother Hares Master?

After a long silence Hares Master told Kobej to forget about all this. What was the point of it? What good would it do? It was useless.

"Why shouldn't I talk about it?" Kobej blamed Hares Master again. "Why are you keeping quiet?" If he had been in Master's place, Kobej went on, he would have smashed everything to the ground by now. That's what Hares should do.

Hares's smile just enraged him more. "Why are you smiling? Have I said anything wrong?" He paused and then said he wanted Master's advice on something.

"About what?"

"You know Pocha?"

"Which Pocha?" Master didn't know him.

Pocha from three villages away. Kobej told him that Pocha had approached him with a proposal a few days ago and now he was sending a messenger every single day to hear what Kobej thought about it.

Hares was curious. "What is this proposal of Pocha's?"

Kobej smiled. "Pocha has set up a dacoit gang. They're doing good business. Pocha wants me to join his gang." He had promised Kobej a good position. Kobej would not have to worry about money any more.

Flabbergasted, Hares Master stared at Kobej.

"Why are you looking at me like that?" Kobej felt uneasy.

"You're going to be an armed robber?"

Kobej was furious. "No rice in the belly . . . "

Hares tried to explain, over and over again, what a bad idea this was. Kobej hadn't fought a war to become a criminal!

"Why did I fight, then?"

Hares had no direct answer to that. He repeated, this wasn't right, wasn't right, not this. Why robbery? Kobej should find something else, anything else.

Kobej wasn't angry anymore. As if without hope, he nodded. "Yes. It won't be right to become a dacoit. I've been asking you to do something for me. You can't. You won't do anything for me, but if I try to do something for myself, you give me that look . . . "

Hares Master went off to Dhaka two days later. He was going to try and see if he could get some governmental assistance for the school. He wanted to turn it into a high school eventually, but right now it was urgent to obtain a regular government grant.

Also, he was going to try to get stipends approved for the villagers who had suffered damages and loss during the war. It was best to deal with such things directly, not through an intermediary. No one else would be able to present their case as convincingly as they could themselves. Who else knew their situation better?

Hares told Kobej repeatedly that he would be back within a few days. He assured Kobej that he would make some arrangement or the other. He was going to personally meet the big leaders. Surely they would understand the situation here! So Kobej should be patient and calm for a while.

Kobej told him to make sure to tell the government about the *ganj* leader. He was a most unsavoury character. The government should know. "And don't come back until you've arranged something for me, I'm warning you."

Hares Master returned after a week. He looked despondent and without hope. He didn't want to talk. Kobej pressed him. "Why so quiet? Tell me."

Hares tried to smile. He would tell Kobej everything. He would, he just needed a little time.

Kobej wasn't amenable. He wanted to know right now. At his insistence, Hares Master was finally forced to open up. No, nothing had worked out. The government officials were all terribly busy. They couldn't spare any time for an outsider. Still, after much effort, Hares had managed to meet a couple of them briefly. The government people had demanded to know whether they were expected to take care of everything all by themselves. They were right. How many things could they attend to? It wasn't as if they were whiling their time away. They were hard at work, day and night. It wouldn't do for people to become impatient and get irked at the slightest delay. They held no magic lamp in their hands that would solve all problems overnight. The problems would be solved—in time.

One leader had, however, shouted at Hares Master. Why were they bringing all these niggling little problems to the capital? These should be settled locally. And was the government supposed to go and check on every house that had been burned down? Did the government have nothing better to do? Hares Master had then brought up the subject of the school and asked for assistance. He had been told that everything would be taken care of in good time, through the proper channels. The poor among the freedom fighters would also receive some aid from the government. But that would most certainly require some more time.

"More time!" Kobej said. "When will the right time come? When we're dead?" He wanted to know if Hares had lodged a complaint against the *ganj* leader. When Hares shook his head, Kobej was angry. "Have you joined forces now with that bastard?" Hares merely smiled, enraging Kobej even further. He told Hares not to smile, for it was making him lose his temper.

Suddenly Hares Master seemed to lose his temper as well. He said he didn't actually believe most of what the government people had told him. They weren't really helping anyone unless the people in question belonged to the ruling party.

Kobej was surprised. Why wouldn't they want to help people? Even if they didn't belong to the government's political party, surely they belonged to the government's country!

"Indeed," Hares said grimly. "But who will tell the government that?"

"Why didn't you tell them?"

"You won't understand, Kobej. Not everything can be said."

"Hah! Just give me the chance. You'll see if I can say it or not."

Hares Master smiled.

"You're smiling again?"

Hares laughed this time. "Apparently the government has no money."

"So much money in everyone's hands and the government has none?"

"That's what I hear."

"Where did Shafiqur get all that money?"

Hares Master smiled and went quiet.

Kobej smiled too and said, "I think then Shafiqur must be a government person." After pausing a moment, he volunteered, "I gave Shafiqur a good thrashing."

"Gave him a thrashing? Why?" Master asked casually. But he got alarmed as soon as it sank in. "What are you saying, Kobej? Why did you beat up Shafiqur?"

Kobej said dispassionately, "Because he was asking for it."

Why? What had he done that was so bad? Hadn't Hares pleaded with Kobej to stay calm and keep his head for a few days?

"You did. But I had no choice."

Kobej told Hares Master the whole story. It had happened two days ago. He had heard screams coming from Akmal Pradhan's house. There was often an uproar in that house these days. Shafiqur and his gang were living it up. But the noise on that day sounded different. Curious, Kobej had strolled over. He had heard a woman's voice, screaming and then weeping. That was when Kobej had entered the house.

Kobej went silent for a few moments when he got to this point in his story. A young woman was weeping her heart out inside. Kobej said that as soon as he set eyes on her he was sure Shafiqur had brought her there for some fun. "And you beat him up?" An angry Hares Master wanted to know.

Shafiqur had brought women to the house before too, to have fun along with his gang. Why hadn't Kobej beaten him up then? Hares Master's allegation wasn't wrong. Ever since they had turned Akmal Pradhan's home into a club, Shafiqur and his friends from the *ganj* had brought in women quite frequently. They drank liquor all night and created a disturbance. Everyone in the village knew. But no one had taken even a single step to investigate. Nobody dared ask him any questions or to tell him not to indulge in debauchery in the village.

Everyone knew Shafiqur had a gun.

Why hadn't he thought it necessary to go there earlier? This question kept Kobej silent for quite a while. Then he replied that he hadn't felt the need. He had gone there two days ago because, Kobej informed Hares, Shafiqur had forced the young woman.

"How do you know that?"

"You can tell," Kobej said. "That's not hard to understand. You can tell just by looking at the girl."

Very well, her face told the story. But even if Shafiqur had forced someone, it was between the two of them. They would work it out for themselves. Why did Kobej have to poke his nose in? Hares Master was dissatisfied. Kobej stared at Hares Master. He couldn't say anything at first.

Gradually the expression on his face changed. In a frigid voice he said, "Let Shafiqur bring over a whore from a whorehouse. I won't say a thing. But if he tries to force a girl just because it pleases him, I'm not going to keep quiet, that's not going to happen."

Hares Master sighed and shook his head. "I understand. But you'd better understand this as well: Shafiqur won't let this pass."

"I'm not letting it pass either."

"You won't win."

"Why not? You'll be on my side."

Hares Master smiled wanly. It made no difference whether he took Kobej's side or not. It made no difference at all.

Hares Master's prediction, that Shafiqur wouldn't let Kobej off, turned out to be true. The very next day, there was a small incident. Kobej wasn't in the village, so Shafiqur's gang couldn't find him. They stood in the middle of the village and fired into the sky. They directed profanities at Kobej. They said they were going to feed his body to vultures. They claimed Kobej had been a collaborator during the war, alongside Akmal Pradhan. It was merely out of generosity that they had left him alone so far.

When he returned in the afternoon and heard about it, Kobej was beside himself with fury. "They called me what? They called me a collaborator? Shafiqur called *me* a collaborator?"

Hares Master tried to calm him down but failed. Kobej said he was going to teach Shafiqur, as well as that uncle of his at the *ganj*, a lesson.

Was Hares Master with him or not?

Hares hesitated and said they shouldn't do anything rash.

"You don't have to support me." Kobej smiled faintly. "I'll take care of it myself."

Hares Master told him that such hotheaded madness would only make things worse.

Kobej laughed. He wasn't a coward like Hares. Did Hares know what Pocha the dacoit had told him?

Hares didn't know.

Why would he? He didn't want to hear or know anything. Kobej told him bitterly that he couldn't tolerate such virtuousness. Hares hadn't been like this during the war. Kobej got angrier as he talked. He had visited Pocha. Pocha had told him everything. A month ago, the *ganj* leader had received a large shipment of relief goods. He had distributed just a fraction of the supplies to the people who needed it, storing the rest in a warehouse. Now he was selling it all in the open market.

Hares Master's jaw dropped. "Is that true?"

Kobej said, "What difference does it make?" What difference did it make to Hares Master whether this was true or not?

"He didn't tell me any of this," Hares Master said. "The leader just hid the whole thing from me."

"Why would he want to tell you?" Kobej chuckled. "The leader knows quite well it makes no difference whether he tells you or not."

Hares Master smiled. "Why are you talking to me like this, Kobej?"

Kobej didn't answer. He said that Pocha had decided to raid the leader's warehouse within a few days and Kobej was going to be part of the gang. But before that, this afternoon actually, he was going to visit the *ganj*. He was going to take care of Shafiqur. He was going to ask the leader to explain what had happened to all the relief goods that had been sent for them. He was going to tell them he wanted to see all of that relief being distributed in their village by tomorrow. Then he would come back and set himself up in Akmal Pradhan's house. He wasn't going to budge an inch.

Hares grabbed his hand. "Don't do it, Kobej. Don't do it."

"Then tell me what I should do."

Hares had no answer.

"Are you with me?"

Hares didn't say anything.

"Tell me if you are. You don't have to be. I can do this by myself."

Hares couldn't persuade him to abandon his plans.

Kobej did go. By himself. He returned after creating a huge commotion. Unharmed. When he was back, he recounted to Hares exactly what he had told the leader and Shafiqur. He had threatened and insulted the leader in front of everyone. He had said exactly what he pleased. The leader's men were itching to have a go at him. But the leader had stopped them. The leader had actually not had the guts to stand up to him. Kobej laughed at Hares Master and said, "So? You see how it is?"

Three days later, the police arrested Kobej. A relative of Ramjan Sheikh's had filed a case against him for Sheikh's murder.

The case went on for about six months. There was no one on Kobej's side. Ramjan Sheikh's side had the support of many people. Everyone was seemingly a close relative of Ramjan Sheikh's and an eyewitness to the incident. But Kobej had never seen any of those people anywhere near Ramjan Sheikh.

The court appointed a lawyer for Kobej. But Kobej was incapable of standing in the dock and giving a coherent account of anything.

When Hares Master went to visit him in jail on the day before the judgment was delivered, surprisingly, Kobej began to weep. "Master, you *will* save me?"

Hares Master had no answer for Kobej.

The next day, the sentence was announced. Due to the overwhelming weight of evidence, Kobej was sentenced to fourteen years in prison for the murder of Ramjan Sheikh.

The Present

Suddenly there was a loud boom. Barely had the echoes from the first explosion dissipated when several more sounded. There had been no disturbances in this neighbourhood all this time, although the threat of danger had existed. Now the constant explosions indicated that the danger had arrived. The thin crowd on the streets disappeared within seconds. People ran helter-skelter. A few groans reached his ears. But they only reached him—he paid no attention. He observed that he was isolated now. There was no one anywhere near him. Those who had surrounded him all this while, praising him, were nowhere to be seen now. He stood all by himself in the middle of a huge, empty space. Like a fool. He felt afraid; he grew afraid; he became afraid. Fear made him grow smaller and smaller and smaller. At this point in the dream, Akmal Pradhan woke up. His sleep was shattered, like the thin film on milk being ripped apart. His sleep was shattered, he woke up, but he wasn't calm. As if he couldn't understand whether he was even here or not. As if his body were an inert, inanimate object and his mind was enclosed in a thick fog. Time passed.

Slowly, he shifted his right hand. Yes, he could feel it. His hand was there, in the right place, attached to his body. He felt better. One by one, he moved his left hand and then his feet. None of them felt numb. So he sat up. Only then did he realise that his whole body was drenched in sweat. Even when he ran his fingers through his hair, he felt perspiration. He sighed, secretly, as if hiding it from himself. There was no air in the room. Perhaps that was why, even though he kept his sigh secret, he felt its lingering presence in the room.

Then, when he felt as if his sigh was right there beside him, he shook his head in anger. He climbed out of bed. He stood beside the window. Outside, a wan, static afternoon. Did afternoon dreams come true? Or was it only the dreams from *subah sadiq*, the dawn twilight, that held true? He couldn't recall. One after another, he looked at every single object within view outside. Then he looked away. He continued to stare, dazed, but not in any particular direction. Why *did* this happen? Why did this happen? Why did these dreams come? Many years had passed since the time that was the backdrop to those dreams. He knew that even those who had been there had forgotten everything by now.

But why couldn't he evade these dreams? Why did they ambush him in the midst of his peaceful sleep? Why did they perturb him so much and so frequently, as they had done right now?

He felt angry and the anger grew. How shameful, he wouldn't even be able to tell anyone about his dream. He had a wife, he had sons and daughters, he had friends and family, but there was no one he was close to. He knew that even if he had someone like that, he still wouldn't have been able to tell them about the dream. This was not a dream to be shared. This was a dream—a nightmare—to be concealed, to fear that someone would find out. It would place him in such a humiliating position. He would be laughed at in secret, behind his back, who knew for how long. This country did not lack for people ready to laugh at others at the slightest provocation.

So he kept it shut up within himself. But it caused great discomfort and distress. How good it would be if he could somehow make sure these nightmares no longer plagued him. But that wasn't going to happen. He knew of no such way. So all he could do was keep these terrifying nightmares walled in. Sometimes it surprised him. He had so many other things in his life. Enjoyable events, joyful events, happy events. Why did none of those show up in his dreams? Or, fine, even if none of those showed up in his dreams, there could be other things that visited him in sleep. For instance, he could dream he was sitting in a heavenly bower surrounded by houris. Or he could dream he was gazing skywards and it was raining gold. Or that all the villagers, and even a few people from the neighbouring villages, were bowing humbly to him. But no, none of those dreams awaited him in his sleep.

His thoughts made him angry again and his anger was unrestrained now. It kept growing until, finally, a sliver of a smile appeared on his face. There was an arbitration scheduled for this afternoon. Akmal Pradhan, it was needless to say, would be the one to sit in judgment. He had decided on the sentence a long time ago. In fact, it would be more truthful to say that the arbitration was being held so he could pass this particular sentence.

He knew—this growing rage that he had right now would be assuaged this afternoon, once he announced his judgment. But suddenly the thought occurred to him, was it the arbitration this afternoon, the fact that he was to pass judgment, that had brought on that dream just now? But why should that be? He had conducted many such *shalish* in the past. These dreams hadn't attacked him then; they had not disturbed his sleep. Had the dreams come today because it was Hares Master on trial? Perhaps, Akmal Pradhan thought, perhaps that was what it was.

As he thought about these things, Akmal Pradhan grew pensive. He felt sad, a sorrow he couldn't evade. Sometimes this happened—he would feel sad, grow preoccupied, for no apparent reason. Was it for no reason? He had tried examining it once or twice. It seemed to come for no reason. He lacked for nothing. He could get whatever he wanted. He had money, intelligence; he could fulfill any desire. It took a while sometimes—but he succeeded. For instance, Hares Master's *shalish*. For a long time, he had been trying to organise some sort of a trial to pass judgment on him. Finally, it was happening. If sometimes things happened differently from the way he wanted, he had the capability of making them turn his way. Take how he had gradually cornered Hares Master and manipulated the situation to his own advantage. Then why did he feel sad? For no reason—what else could he tell himself?

He didn't want to think about it, but he knew that the memories of the horrible months after 1971 were the reason for his occasional pensiveness. That was what brought on the sadness. And those nightmares that pursued him. But he had no reason to cling to the memories of those terrible months. Those bad days were gone, they were finished. There was no more reason to live in fear, to bow and scrape in front of anyone else. Still, he couldn't avoid it—sometimes he just felt despondent. At times, he hung his head in pure shame. What could he call it now besides 'needless'?

A faint smile appeared on his face once more. There was no harm admitting it to himself—this thought made him smile. Those had been bad days, extremely bad. Remembering them damaged his confidence. He felt restless, out of control. Like right now, he was restless again. He emerged from his room to calm himself down. He paced along the long veranda that ran in front of his room. He ordered a cup of tea for himself and returned to his bedroom.

These days, he wanted a cup of tea rather frequently. A rich man's habit. He laughed at himself. Did this mean he had become a rich man? If a rich man was someone who didn't have enough room to store his money, then that was him. His wealth had not been made in a day. It was an edifice he had built penny by penny. He had always had money. Then, near the end of 1971, the absence of Ramjan Sheikh had given him a great opportunity. Most of his property had been seized after December 16, 1971, however. He had had to reacquire them. But that hadn't been much of a struggle. A minor nuisance, that was all. The bigger problem had had to do with Hares Master. When Pradhan had finally returned to the village, he had found out that Hares Master had taken over all the land that Pradhan had managed to grab during 1971. Hares hadn't exactly taken it over—rather, he had distributed it among some of the villagers. They were farming it together and then sharing the harvest.

It had made his blood boil. Those *fokirs* had never had the guts to even look him in the face. And now they were ploughing his fields, taking home his harvest! He had got into a big argument with Hares Master over this. He had demanded an explanation from Hares Master. Had the country been liberated so that people could just grab the land of others?

He was kept busy over the land that he had acquired during the war. He got new deeds and documents issued, made many visits to the police and the courts. There were a few others in the village who had been eyeing those plots of land. They had all been vengeful because Hares Master hadn't allowed any of them to take them over. Every single one of them supported Akmal Pradhan. Hares Master's influence over the village had decreased by then. So none of that nonsense of a cooperative movement had survived. The little resistance that Hares Master and his group had put together at the very last moment had been smashed to smithereens by Kobej.

TEN

Kobej was a monstrous figure then. A handful of people had shown up to resist Pradhan's attempt at land-grabbing. Kobej took care of all of them by himself. He beat them up like a madman. Several heads were cracked open and a few arms broken. One man lost an eye. Kobej abused Hares Master in the filthiest of language. Akmal Pradhan had understood the truth at that moment: Kobej wasn't merely trying to get the job done, he was also trying to prove his allegiance to Akmal Pradhan. He had smiled inwardly. What harm would it do? In fact, that was exactly what he had wanted—that Kobej be loyal to him. He had been loyal in the past, let him be so again. It was only during this brief period in between that some madness had possessed Kobej.

No, Akmal Pradhan would never forget Kobej's face that day, not as long as he lived. Kobej had woken him up in the middle of the night. His clothes were bloodstained, his hair dishevelled, his eyes bloodshot. He said he'd done it, he'd killed Ramjan Sheikh. It had been such wonderful news. He couldn't decide whether to hug Kobej in elation or carry him on his shoulders. What did Kobej want? Akmal Pradhan had already agreed to money and land. He wouldn't have said no had Kobej wanted anything more.

But a strange smile had blossomed on Kobej's face. Akmal Pradhan hadn't understood the meaning of that smile, but it had scared him. Why was Kobej behaving this way? Why was he giving him these peculiar looks? He hadn't understood that Kobej had undergone a great change. Kobej had told him incomprehensibly that, no, he hadn't got rid of Ramjan Sheikh for money or land. Why, then? The question had occurred to him at once. But he hadn't got the chance to ask it. He had had to flee from Kobej's attack before that. Memories of that night still made him tremble. Kobej had leapt towards him, about to grab him with both hands. Pradhan had sensed danger only moments before and had barely managed to avoid Kobej's outstretched arms. He had shoved Kobej to the floor and run out. Outside, standing at a safe distance, he had screamed and screamed. All these were like still images of successive moments.

Lying on the floor, Kobej had realised that Pradhan's shouts were dangerous. He had got up and rushed outside. Even though he hadn't been able to pinpoint Pradhan's location, he had shouted at him. "You and your fucking Pakistan, I'll fuck you up too, you son of a bitch." He had run into the darkness and disappeared. Pradhan had been left trembling.

The next day, Akmal Pradhan was in some trouble. Who had killed Ramjan Sheikh, who? The Pakistani army officer was roaring. Pradhan had said, without blinking an eye, "Why, who else can it be? It has to be those infidels." This hadn't satisfied the officer though. Ramjan Sheikh's men had instigated him. They had mentioned Kobej and a few even claimed to have seen him. The officer hadn't believed them in the end though. Perhaps that was because of Ali Akkas's support of Pradhan.

In fact, the officer hadn't even asked where Kobej was.

There was another reason, Pradhan realised over the next few days. The officer was no fool. It wasn't important to him whether Akmal Pradhan's man had killed Ramjan Sheikh or not. Already the *mukti bahini* had launched a small attack. The officer knew that such attacks would only increase. So he needed support, he needed men he could rely on. Ramjan Sheikh was gone, but Akmal Pradhan was still there, and so it was Akmal Pradhan he needed. Otherwise, it would be difficult to obtain information about this locality and the surrounding areas, or to get help on minor tasks. So the officer dismissed Ramjan Sheikh's murder as inconsequential and drew Akmal Pradhan into his inner circle.

Akmal Pradhan didn't fret over why the officer was doing this. He had no need to worry himself. He busied himself sorting out his future. Opportunity knocked on the door only once or twice in life. Many fools never even noticed. He was no fool. He knew which knocks represented opportunity waiting at the door. He also knew that it only came once or twice. So he didn't let the opportunity opened up by Kobej go to waste.

It wasn't just the judicious use of opportunity; the knowledge that he was the constant companion of a Pakistani army officer also brought him great mental peace. He did, of course, have to work very hard as well. Akmal Pradhan knew that he had to not only fill the vacuum left by Ramjan Sheikh, but also prove himself worthier than Sheikh. That was how he proceeded. He supplied the officer with regular news and information, both true and false. He decimated a few more families in the village. He extended his sphere of influence to surrounding villages as well. Seven or eight villages came under his control eventually. Ali Akkas and he were a strong team. The Pakistani officer relied on them unconditionally. Was there no danger amidst all this? There was danger every step of the way. He paid no attention. If he hid himself, if he lagged behind because he was afraid, he would accomplish nothing in this life. And where did danger not exist? He could die even in his sleep. So a little risk, yes, but the gains were great. Not only money or land, but a monopoly of influence, the respect accorded to a leader—all of this kept him absorbed in working against the dismantling of Pakistan, as the ever-watchful guard against the kafirs and infidels.

Of course he thought of Kobej sometimes. Now and then, he felt Kobej's absence deeply. He couldn't understand why Kobej had behaved the way he had. Why, Kobej, why did you do it? He couldn't answer the question, couldn't resolve the astonishment. Why had Kobej suddenly gone mad? If it wasn't for land or money, why had he murdered Ramjan Sheikh? The bigger question was: why had Kobej attacked him as well? Why, when he couldn't get him, had Kobej hurled that threat into the darkness, about fucking Pakistan and fucking Akmal Pradhan? Did it mean that Kobej had not approved of the absolute loyalty to Pakistan that they had adopted? That's what it seemed like to Akmal Pradhan, but he couldn't quite bring himself to believe it. What did Kobej understand, anyway?

Or had Kobej begun to understand everything in secret, without Pradhan's knowledge? Perhaps that was it. He had praised the courage of the *mukti bahini* to the skies and he had been angry with Ramjan Sheikh. But then would Kobej have killed Ramjan Sheikh for this alone? And would he have attacked the very man who had been his shelter for so long? It didn't add up. Pradhan had made covert enquiries about Kobej's whereabouts from time to time. He had discovered nothing. He had never been angry with Kobej. It was strange but true. Instead he had grown extremely curious. When he couldn't uncover any information on his whereabouts, he began to wonder: had Kobej joined the *mukti*? If that had happened, Akmal Pradhan thought to himself, then there was absolutely no doubt about it, Kobej had gone stark raving mad. However, he hadn't been able to spend too much time on Kobej. He was well on his way to going mad himself. How many things was he supposed to take care of? What with torching the homes of infidels, looting their possessions, claiming their land, managing his team of *razakar*s and holding informal trial sessions, he barely had time to draw breath. He had even less time as the year came to an end. He really did feel he was going mad. Because by then, the *mukti bahini* had gained considerable ground.

The freedom fighters were holding their own against the Pakistani armed forces. In many areas, the Pakistani army had lost ground to them and was in disarray. The influence of the *mukti bahini* was growing day by day, everywhere. Even Akmal Pradhan had begun to feel the pressure and was confounded. Allah's faithful, the Pakistani army, was losing out to the infidel *mukti bahini*—how could this actually happen? When he asked, Ali Akkas reassured him there was nothing to fear. The Pakistani army would destroy the infidel freedom fighters in just a few more days.

He didn't know whether he should believe it or not. All kinds of rumours, for and against, were blowing in the wind. Some were saying new forces were due to arrive from West Pakistan. These Special Forces were said to live underground. They emerged only at night to fight. No one could win against them. These were the fighters who had seized more than half of India's land during the war between Pakistan and India. Some said the Pakistani soldiers were actually playing a cat-and-mouse game with the boys of the *mukti bahini*. When the time came, they would give the freedom fighters such a walloping, they won't know which way to run. Then there were those whose conjectures ran counter to all of this. Some said it was a matter of just days now before the freedom fighters chopped the Pakistani army into little pieces. Some said the Pakistani soldiers no longer wanted war. They wanted to run away. So as soon as they came up against the *mukti* fighters, they threw down their weapons and surrendered. Some had even fled to Pakistan already.

Which of these were credible and which weren't? Gradually, it seemed to him that the second group was right. Either Ali Akkas was intentionally misleading him or he couldn't read the situation. But Pradhan had. The Pakistani army no longer possessed its earlier verve. The local *razakar* troop fell apart right in front of his eyes. Some of them died and some fled in fear, who knew where! Akmal Pradhan had no difficulty in understanding what all this pointed to, what these indications meant. But what could he do? If the Pakistani army lost the war, then he was done for as well. Would the freedom fighters let him live? Whenever he thought that all this money, this land, all of this would still be here, but only he would be gone, he felt bewildered and lost. He sat down for a second meeting with Ali Akkas. If something like that happened, if the Pakistani army lost the war to the *mukti bahini*, what was Ali Akkas going to do? Ali Akkas couldn't give him a satisfactory answer.

Akmal Pradhan began to organise things when he came home from the meeting. He might have to flee. He had no idea where he could escape to, but he might have to. His main problem was money. Money: he had plenty. He had no worries about his land. No one could loot the land. He wasn't worried about his house, either. No one could take away his house. His worry was about his money and his respect. But respect—it would stay if it was meant to, and if it went, perhaps he would get it back one day. That was the nature of respect. It didn't stay with one person for too long. So he wasn't too worried about respect. He was worried about money. If he had to flee and left cash in the house, he would never get it back when he returned. So he had to take his cash with him.

The problem was how to carry all this cash. He had to make arrangements. He had always been aware of the power conferred by money. More power than could be granted by any Pakistani officer. If anything could save him, it would be the money. He gathered all his cash. He sent off his wife and young son to his in-laws' house with a large bundle of money. He entrusted a large amount with an old friend, a businessman at the *ganj*. The rest, he kept with himself.

He spent the last few days in intense anxiety. One day, right in front of his eyes, the Pakistani army decamped and left the village. He heard that a large troop of freedom fighters had positioned themselves a few villages away. One afternoon, news arrived of heavy fighting nearby. The largest Pakistani army troop in their region had lost that battle. That afternoon, Akmal Pradhan fled the village.

He spent the night at the *ganj*, at the house of his old friend. He sent a secret messenger to the residence of Ali Akkas—but there was no news of him. He managed to pass the night there and started for the city early the next morning. The city wasn't too close to his village. He felt safer there. Two days later, East Pakistan became Bangladesh. He shaved off his carefully cultivated beard. He observed himself for long moments in the mirror and felt relieved. He looked completely different. Lucky that he had thought of shaving his beard. What good would a beard do if he lost his life? If he survived, he could grow his beard back someday. Perhaps the ideology that had prompted the beard would also grow back to full strength one day.

He didn't stay in that city for too long. Nobody knew him here. But the city wasn't all that far from his village. There was always the chance that he would be spotted by someone from the other side. He felt the need to move to an even safer place. Four days later, he started for Dhaka.

ELEVEN

When Akmal Pradhan reached Dhaka, he realised it wasn't as safe as he had assumed. There were plenty of people there and it was easy to disappear in the crowd. But there were risks. People like him, who had supported Pakistan during the war, were being captured one by one. Many were surrendering. For one moment, he thought he should do the same. Surrender and say he made a mistake, please forgive me. But what would happen to all his money? What if he was forgiven but his money wasn't! And who knew if it was a better deal to surrender or not. He decided to just hide and survive for as long as he could.

Six months went by. He didn't just sit idle these six months. He looked for a way in. There was always a way in. There was always a chink that could be opened up. Once you located that chink, you had to angle your way in. It took him four more months to find that chink. By then, the situation was easing somewhat. The good news was that the country was in bad shape. Every single member of the ruling party was so busy with their own problems that they had no time to look elsewhere. Many magic tricks were being performed while those in power looked away. By then, Pradhan had located a distant relative who had a close relationship with the ruling party. An efficient man. He told Pradhan directly—he was busy, very busy, taking care of his future. Akmal Pradhan had already had that experience. He understood his relative's situation easily.

It was through the distant relative that, one day, he reached as far as a minor leader in the ruling party. And then he met a mid-level leader, who said, "Yes, I've heard of you. You provided a lot of support to the Pakistani army."

Pradhan smiled and said that he had supplied information in secret to the *mukti bahini* and made sure that innocent people in the village weren't tortured. And, yes, he was the one who, at the risk of his own life, had killed the Pakistani informer and collaborator Ramjan Sheikh. The mid-level leader said, "Hmm, that's what everyone claims these days."

The mid-level leader's words didn't discourage him. He knew what they indicated. He made sure everyone was kept happy. The distant relative, the minor leader, the mid-level leader. At an opportune moment, as if he really hadn't wanted to but was saying it anyway, he mentioned that he was very influential in his village. People listened to him. His orders were carried out. The leader could use him to get things done if he so wanted.

The money and those words did their work. But he was required to invest more. Cash flowed out like water down a slope. Let it. If money didn't flow out, how would he open the channels to let it flow in? Pradhan didn't spend money on these three alone, but on many others as well. He felt the power of money anew. He witnessed that money was not only more powerful than senior officers of the Pakistani army, it was actually more powerful than those who claimed that they had triumphed over the Pakistani army and liberated the country.

Although the situation eased, he stayed on in Dhaka for six more months. He realised that returning to the village too soon might be cause for danger. While in Dhaka, he began collecting information on the village and the *ganj*. He found out that Ramjan Sheikh's house, and his own as well, had been seized by the *ganj* leader. He also learned that Hares Master had taken over his land, distributed it and begun a cooperative movement. He already knew that Kobej had joined the freedom fighters, had fought alongside Hares Master, and was in jail serving a sentence for murdering Ramjan Sheikh. He received more news from the *ganj*. Ali Akkas was thriving. Apparently his son had joined the freedom fighters, so he hadn't suffered any consequences for his own role during the war. Akmal Pradhan had laughed—when had Ali Akkas's son joined the *mukti*? Must be a member of the Sixteenth Division, he thought, all those men claiming to be freedom fighters after the war had been won. He began corresponding with Ali Akkas. He wrote to his old friend, who was holding on to his cash for him. When he got positive signals from both, he returned to the *ganj*.

He tested the waters for the first few days. When he felt certain he was in no danger, he began the process of getting his affairs back in order. First, he needed to take back his house. But that was in the possession of the *ganj* leader, who had no interest in what the party leaders in Dhaka had promised Akmal Pradhan. He was the man in charge here and things would run the way he wanted them to. But Akmal Pradhan was not discouraged. Ali Akkas was the leader's brother; through Akkas, Pradhan kept up his efforts. He argued that the leader would still retain possession of Ramjan Sheikh's house, so there should be no problem in returning his. If the *ganj* leader relinquished Pradhan's house, he could count on his support for anything in the future.

That worked to some extent. The rest was done by the Marwari businessman Tejaram. Tejaram actually lived and conducted most of his business on the other side of the border. But now he had become quite influential on this side as well. One of the people he had done business with before 1971 was Ramjan Sheikh. Sheikh's absence had not meant his business had suffered, though. He transported enormous quantities of goods to both sides of the border every day. He knew all about Akmal Pradhan. Since Ramjan Sheikh was no more, he needed Akmal Pradhan to ensure control over the movement of his goods, not only in this village but in the surrounding villages as well. So Tejaram extended his efforts on Pradhan's behalf.

One afternoon, the three of them sat down together: Akmal Pradhan, the *ganj* leader and Tejaram. Tejaram had probably spoken to the *ganj* leader already. The leader agreed to relinquish his hold on Akmal Pradhan's house. He also expressed some remorse at all these misunderstandings with Akmal Pradhan. And he made a small promise. Of course he would look out for Tejaram's business interests when needed. He would help Pradhan when necessary. In return, Tejaram should make sure his needs were met. Akmal Pradhan returned home two days later.

Certain arrangements had already been made. He faced no discomfort. As planned, a small procession traversed the village soon after his arrival. Participants informed the villagers that things were very bad right now, that every household was in poverty and now was the time a leader like Akmal Pradhan was sorely needed.

Akmal Pradhan took a little more time, though. He had a to-do list ready. He would get to the items one by one—there was no rush. He helped some villagers generously. Alongside, he also began issuing instructions. But he realised how difficult it was to not have someone loyal by his side. He felt Kobej's absence keenly.

It would be so much easier to get things done with someone loyal like Kobej by his side. The thought made him chuckle. Could he still think of Kobej as loyal?

He could, he decided after thinking it through. Kobej had gone off his head and made a small mistake in 1971, without knowing or understanding the truth of things. He couldn't brand Kobej disloyal just because of that. People went overboard some-times when they became hotheaded—it wasn't unusual. He'd seen it in 1971, hadn't he? So hotheaded that they split the country into two! Let them—his regret over this was disappearing grad-ually. Now he needed Kobej by his side. But since Kobej had lost his head once, he could do it again. Before Akmal Pradhan accepted him back, he should sound him out carefully. He went to visit Kobej in prison. When Kobej saw him, he just stared.

"How are you, Kobej?" he asked.

"You can see how I am." Kobej tried to smile.

"Yes, I can. How did this happen? Why are you in prison?"

"You think I'm here by choice?" Kobej was aggrieved. "They put me in here!"

"Who put you in prison?"

Kobej was silent.

"When do you come out?"

That was a long way away. Kobej laughed. He said he wasn't too badly off, actually. At least he had no worries about getting two meals a day.

Akmal Pradhan sat opposite him and pretended to ponder over things with a worried face. He glanced affectionately at Kobej several times. Then he wanted to know: should he try to get Kobej released from prison? It would be hard, but if Kobej wanted it, he would try.

Kobej looked at him as though he couldn't understand a word he was saying.

Akmal Pradhan chided him gently, "Well, why don't you say something?"

"Released?" A slight smile showed momentarily on Kobej's face. He wanted to know what he would do if he were released.

"You'll be with me," Akmal Pradhan said, casually but firmly.

"You'll take me back?" Kobej seemed not to understand a word of what Akmal Pradhan was saying.

"But you *were* with me." A genuine smile surfaced on Akmal Pradhan's face. Kobej was silent for a long while. Maybe he was reminded of that night in 1971. Perhaps he felt some shame. Recovering, he said, "Look, I do want to be with you."

"I know. I'll get you out." Akmal Pradhan paused and said, "Kobej, did you join the *mukti bahini*?"

Kobej looked at him in surprise. He couldn't understand the reason for this sudden question.

Pradhan asked again.

Kobej nodded slightly. Yes, he had joined. And that was why he was now in . . .

"Trouble?" Akmal Pradhan didn't want to hear any of this, he knew already. Lightly, he asked, "I'm the one who sent you to fight with the *mukti*, right?"

Kobej was taken aback. He stared at Akmal Pradhan for a few seconds. Then, slowly, he nodded. Yes, Pradhan was the one who sent him.

"That's what you'll say, right?"

"That's what I'll say," Kobej replied in a steady voice.

"Whom will you say it to? Where will you say it?"

"To anyone you tell me to. Wherever you tell me to."

Akmal Pradhan busied himself securing Kobej's release from prison. He lobbied with the *ganj* leader and with Tejaram, who pulled strings where needed. Kobej, however, was released even before their efforts had culminated. He was one among several hundred prisoners granted release by the government on a special day of celebration. Or maybe Kobej's name had shown up on that list because of the efforts made by the *ganj* leader and Tejaram. Kobej had been a freedom fighter, after all. It was quite all right to lobby with the higher-ups on his behalf.

Akmal Pradhan organised a huge rally to welcome Kobej back. There was also a meeting to felicitate him. Pradhan himself was the chief speaker. He praised the freedom fighter Kobej to the skies. He told everyone that Kobej had played a big role in the liberation of Bangladesh. However, he didn't openly claim that he was responsible for sending Kobej to war. No need to state everything at one go. It could keep. Like a new account in the bank, it could be an asset. To be used in the future, if necessary.

Eventually, Akmal Pradhan didn't need to broadcast that he had sent Kobej to fight the liberation war. Pradhan merely made sure that Kobej was recognised as a major freedom fighter. Then he proceeded to extract his land from Hares Master's farming collective. He could have done it earlier. Hares Master had been a freedom fighter. Once upon a time, he had been a *mukti*, but what power did he wield anymore? Pradhan could have repossessed his land by handing over a small share to the *ganj* leader and then lobbying with the police and the courts. But everything had to be done in its own way. This one was a job for Kobej, the freedom fighter.

Meanwhile, 1974 arrived. Many people died. There was one particular opinion that Akmal Pradhan had been professing carefully in intimate gatherings the past few years. Now he began saying it in public: how had the Pakistan era been any worse than this!

TWELVE

Akmal Pradhan didn't say it these days, though. In fact, he berated those who did. Why should anyone—or even Pradhan himself—say such things! If Bangladesh could be turned into Pakistan, there was no need to say such things at all.

He stood up from his chair. He stood by the window watching the radiance outside die. The afternoon light would now spread everywhere. He moved away from the window and sat on the bed. He was feeling better now. The anxiety that had bothered him ever since he had had the dream was gone. He was feeling much more at ease. Quite cheerful, in fact.

His wife came to ask what he would like with his tea. Every day, he ate a serving of milk curd with his tea. First the milk curd and then, five minutes later, tea with thickened milk. Everyone knew this, but his wife still had to ask every day. The house was full of maids and servants, but she insisted on finding out for herself. When he was in a good mood, he didn't mind. He rather enjoyed his wife's assiduous care. This was what he had always wanted—that people take note of his presence.

Kobej was waiting in the outer room. He had been informed of Kobej's arrival. He knew why Kobej was here. He was in no hurry—Kobej could wait awhile. He ate the curd slowly. He allowed some time to pass. Then he slurped loudly on the tea with thickened milk. He thought of his youngest son.

The eldest among his three sons was studying in the Middle East. That he would enter politics on his return was a done deal. His second son was working. He had studied law, passed some tough exams and had got a government job. His third son—the youngest—was studying at Dhaka University. It had been several years already—there was no saying when he would actually graduate. This youngest son didn't approve of him slurping his tea. When he was present, he objected strongly. Akmal Pradhan laughed. His son had mastered not only a few pages from his books, but also some urban sophistication. Good for him. But what did he know of the joys of slurping hot tea!

To him, it seemed as though life itself surged upwards with every sip. He had already decided that his third son was to go into business. His son was interested as well. If only he had one more son. Sometimes he experienced some regret. If he had another son, he could have sent him into the army. He had thought of this too late. Otherwise he could have sent any one of his three sons into the armed forces. After the three sons, he had had a daughter. He had married her off young. His daughter was a cheeky, brazen girl who had no sense of propriety or shame. She would canoodle with anyone whenever she got a chance. Eventually, she got herself into trouble. How disgraceful it would have been for him if everyone had got to know! He arranged to get rid of it, had his daughter cleansed and married her off in the city. As for the young man who had got her in trouble, Akmal Pradhan laid a trap and made life so difficult for him that he was forced to vanish.

His eldest son shared his daughter's proclivities. The one who was studying in a Middle Eastern country, who was to return and become a politician. Not a single housemaid or female labourer connected to their household escaped his attention. Sometimes he would get them into trouble as well. Pradhan didn't like trouble anymore. He had had enough of it. He wanted to live a trouble-free, anxiety-free life now. Of course, children didn't have to inherit their father's habits. So he had rid himself of all these troubles by sending his son to the Middle East, and by marrying his daughter off. He wanted no more problems. And so, today, Hares Master was on trial.

He finished his tea and got to his feet. He was no longer young—he had crossed fifty. But his health and physique were rock solid. His beard was clipped neatly. People praised his looks. These days, he lined his eyes with kohl regularly. He took care of his voice. He knew a firm timbre could solve many problems. He spoke in a baritone which could take root inside people's heads. They took in the magic of his voice rather than what he actually said.

Kobej was waiting in the drawing room. He was no longer a young man. But he had aged even better than Pradhan. He was still very strong physically. Of course, it was necessary for him to maintain a healthy and strong physique. It wouldn't do not to. When Kobej saw him he stood up with a salam. He responded to the salam and glanced at Kobej out of the corner of his eye. In the past, Kobej used to carry a gun. This was when Pradhan had just returned to the village after the war. He didn't have to say anything to Kobej. Kobej understood that sort of thing back then and still did. He no longer carried a weapon. Why should he, when there was no longer any need? Pradhan didn't have to tell him. When the time came, Kobej stopped on his own. These days, there was nothing to fear even without a gun. There was no one to create problems that might require a gun to resolve. Even Kobej knew this, let alone Pradhan himself.

Still, a certain fear overtook him sometimes. Not always, just occasionally. There was no specific reason for this fear. But a fear that came without a specific cause couldn't always be avoided. During those times, he thought perhaps it would be better if Kobej did carry a gun. What trouble was it to carry one, really? Who knew when a gun would be needed? Best to be prepared.

He had never, however, been able to say this to Kobej. Because then Kobej would know he was afraid. No matter how close Kobej was to him, he couldn't let him see his fear. That would put a crack in Kobej's faith in him. And once a crack opened, it would only get wider.

He paused for a moment in front of Kobej, asking how things were. Kobej nodded. Everything was fine. There were no problems anywhere. He knew this. Still, it made him feel better to hear it from his men. Anyway, it was best to keep abreast of problems and perils. No one knew when danger would spread its wings to take flight.

Akmal Pradhan left his house. He didn't have to tell Kobej to follow him. Pradhan stopped when he was outside. The road stretched out wide in front of him—the minaret of the mosque was in clear view in the distance. The mosque didn't have that minaret originally, he had built it. Behind the mosque was an empty expanse of land. That was where Hares Master's trial was to be held today. When he looked in that direction, when he recalled that he was going to announce his predetermined verdict on Hares Master today, his face lit up with a satisfied smile. He stepped forward, the smile still on his face

He was going to circle around his house once now. He was also going to visit the plots of land that he owned nearby. His house expanded a little bit every year. Just like his land holdings. It took him much longer now to inspect all his land. He had to walk more. Of course, he enjoyed the journey. It felt very good.

He took a few steps forward. As if he were going on a leisurely stroll around his house. But he noted every detail closely. The afternoon's nightmare grew fainter, until it gradually disappeared. His house was sprawling. From one part of the building, he could even see part of his vast land holdings. Yes, vast. Like his presence and position here. No one else had control or right of entry. It was his monopoly. That was why he enjoyed walking around his own land so much. It made clear how much he had grown since 1971.

He returned to the main house after his stroll. Now he was going to eat two boiled eggs and drink a glass of milk. Then he would smoke. This was a new addiction, quite a luxurious affair. His eggs and milk arrived, along with food for Kobej, after he had settled in the drawing room. When he finished his snack, he drew his hookah closer and looked directly at Kobej. Kobej knew what he was supposed to do. He began talking.

He nodded when Kobej finished. Yes, everything seemed fine, Kobej had followed instructions. Still there were some things he should double-check. He asked whether Kobej had informed the police. Kobej knew of Akmal Pradhan's habits, but he was still a bit annoyed. He said he had; he didn't make amateur mistakes. How long did it take to make one, laughed Pradhan. Had the government offices been notified as well? Kobej reported he had taken care of that too.

These arrangements had to be made in advance. Simply for reasons of caution. He was the chairman of the union council, he had the right to hold an arbitration trial. But Akmal Pradhan was averse to any risks and wanted to make sure everyone was involved too. He smiled at Kobej, saying, "This time I'm shoving that bamboo right up Hares Master's arse."

He wouldn't have bothered with such a scheme, but that Hares Master had a bad attitude. He kept harassing Pradhan for no reason. So what if Hares Master had fought in the *mukti bahini* years ago? So what if they had kicked the Pakistani army out of this country? What did any of that matter anymore? Hares Master had become a laughingstock. He was such a bloody fool, he didn't even understand that people were mocking him. If he was just a fool though, he wouldn't have been a problem. The problem was Hares Master didn't realise he was a fool. Although Pradhan could have tolerated even this, if Hares Master had only left him alone.

It was disconcerting to be hounded constantly. Even if Hares Master couldn't actually do anything, he was an annoyance. In any case, could Pradhan really dismiss him as a man of no consequence? He had noticed there were many in the village, even so many years after 1971, who still paid attention to what Hares Master said. His influence also seemed to be growing in the *ganj*. Observing all this, he had decided that this was the time to knock Hares Master to the ground—so hard that he could never stand up again.

First, he told Kobej. He said an enemy should never be allowed to survive. It only meant danger in the future. Kobej asked whether he should take care of Hares Master for good.

But no, that wasn't what Pradhan wanted. Hares Master was so proud of being a freedom fighter during the war—it would be delightful to watch him once his spine was broken. So Pradhan made a plan. He took his time over it. He spent money where needed. He made sure that the emotions of people ran high. Now all that remained was to announce his verdict.

THIRTEEN

It was time for the Maghreb prayers by the time the eggs, milk and tobacco had been consumed. Akmal Pradhan set the nozzle of his hookah down and belched luxuriously. He turned to Kobej and said, "Why don't you go and take care of everything? I'll be along in a few minutes." When Kobej left, Pradhan changed his clothes. Then he walked quickly towards the mosque. The *shalish* was supposed to begin right after the Maghreb prayers. He should get there a little early.

It was probably the arbitration that had drawn a large crowd at the mosque this evening. The courtroom was quite spartan, though: a few chairs, four benches and a few mats spread out.

People would have to sit on the ground if this seating arrangement didn't suffice. The villagers wouldn't object. They knew such trials held ample possibility of entertainment. Kobej and his men had brought in Hares Master. The slightly-built Hares Master looked fearless but anxious in the light of the paraffin lamp. He looked in turn at the people seated on the chairs, the mats and the benches. He didn't throw a glance at Akmal Pradhan even by mistake.

Akmal Pradhan thought Hares Master was trying to pretend he couldn't care less about Pradhan's presence, but was actually scared. Not looking at him directly was a sign of this fear. Akmal Pradhan laughed in his head. He cleared his throat and stood up. He didn't look at Hares Master. He looked at the men sitting on the chairs, the benches and the mats. In his deep voice, he addressed them, "Brothers . . . "

The evening had spread everywhere. It seemed to Akmal Pradhan that even the bright light of the paraffin lamp couldn't dispel the darkness. Instead, the two had melded to make the surroundings ghostly. He cleared his throat again. "Brothers . . . " How strange, as soon as he uttered the word "brothers," he was reminded of that afternoon's nightmare. He wanted to forget that particular dream. He stopped. In a louder voice, he began, "Those who act against the dictates of the sharia . . . " But no, before he could finish, his afternoon nightmare reappeared, shimmering in front of his eyes.

He felt unsettled. Somehow, Hares Master sensed his unease. Suddenly, astonishing everyone, he jumped up and shouted, "You! How dare you sit in judgment of me! You son of a bitch, you were a Pakistani army collaborator . . . !"

Hares Master's audacity stunned him. Had the man gone mad? Akmal Pradhan shouted in a rage, "Me? A collaborator? Who told you that?"

"I don't need anyone to tell me! No one needs to be told!" Master roared in return.

Akmal Pradhan roared back, "Ask Kobej! Who sent him to the liberation war? Who sent him to fight?"

Hares Master looked at Kobej with a piercing gaze.

Kobej couldn't care less. In an impassive voice, he reported that he had joined the *mukti bahini* because Akmal Pradhan had instructed him to. Therefore, Akmal Pradhan was also a freedom fighter. Akmal Pradhan had done his work while remaining within the country.

Hares Master was furious. "You're calling *him* a freedom fighter, Kobej? Kobej, you're not a human being, Kobej, you're a boot-licking dog!"

Without another word, Kobej launched himself at Hares Master. Blinded by rage, he punched Hares again and again. He screamed like a madman. He was going to pull out Hares Master's tongue. He was going to chop him into little pieces and throw him into the river. Hares Master could not stand straight or even sit up by the time Kobej's own companions finally pulled him away.

Akmal Pradhan felt a keen enjoyment on seeing Kobej in this role. This was how minor leaders, the low-ranking ones who whined on and on about morality, should be treated. They shouted so loudly about ethics that they grew deaf and were unable to accept present-day truths. They didn't want to submit.

So this was how they ought to be taught a lesson. This wasn't an issue with major or big leaders though. They understood the present. They knew which way the winds blew, they knew that politics required different kinds of action. One could compromise and reach an understanding with them.

Akmal Pradhan had not planned to claim that he himself had been a freedom fighter, that he had been the one to send Kobej to the war.

But Hares Master had begun to shout at him and called him a Pakistani collaborator! Let him—it made no difference now. Not one person would desert Pradhan to support Hares Master. Still, he had said it; he had just had his little fun with Hares Master, that was all. Pradhan cleared his throat again. Hares Master lay half collapsed on the ground. He had probably already learned his lesson. Still, since this was a trial, a sentence had to be pronounced. Pradhan let his voice rise. He didn't allow the afternoon's nightmare anywhere near him.

It hadn't been just a dream though. One evening in 1971, he really had set up a trial for two young men. They had been captured and brought from two villages away. Their crime: they might or might not have had some sort of connection with the *mukti bahini*. That day too he had been responsible for passing judgment. But before he could begin the sentencing, there had been a fusillade of bullets. The *mukti bahini* was attacking. No, the freedom fighters hadn't even been targeting them. They had been shooting from a distance, based on surmise.

But that attack had ruined everything. Everyone had fled. He himself had escaped as well. He had raced away, unable to breathe. The terror, the fear—it still made him tremble.

But now he had no fear. There was no one now to stop him from pronouncing judgment. He knew there would be no clamour of protest. He wouldn't need to flee. Even if a commotion broke out, it would be mere sound, not bullets. It would be a noise without consequence. Kobej alone would be enough to smash that noise to smithereens.

●